GW00857382

First Published ir
By Castle............. ....

ISBN: 9798696214627

Cover designed by Selina Crutcher

Photographs by David Fulford

Facebook: Mica Ford - Forest Adventures

ABOUT THE AUTHOR

Mica Ford has lived most of her life in the beautiful New Forest in southern England. Brought up on a dairy and then chicken farm by adventurous parents, she attended Swansea University before marrying and becoming the mother of three lively children. Now a grandmother, she has combined her love of horses, reading and writing with a busy life.

She and her husband renovated several houses in England before embarking on their most ambitious venture: converting a French barn into a second home.

MICA FORD is also the author of a series of children's books, following the adventures of three sisters riding their ponies in the New Forest:

Forest Summer
Forest Festivities
Forest Rescue
Forest Rustlers

Facebook author page: Mica Ford - Forest Adventures

Love at First Sight

Chapter 1

My family loves France. As a young girl I had accompanied my parents on their boat through the French canals, then when David and I married and had children, we'd travelled the length and breadth of the country over a period of twenty years. We stayed in semi-converted barns, stone houses, gites and mobile homes. We camped, towed our caravan, flew and drove across its beautiful mountains, gorges and coasts; I have even 'sailed' many of its amazing network of canals. For many years our desire was to buy a little piece of France. Not a chateau, even

though we looked longingly at them, but something we could call our own. Over the years we made numerous forays into the finances and practicalities of owning a villa with a swimming pool in the south, a mobile home on a
child friendly camp site, an apartment on the coast, or a barn to convert. You name it, we investigated it.

David rather fancied living in France permanently; something to do with the roads empty of traffic and the slower pace of life, and just possibly the wine. But the demands of earning our daily crust as well as looking after our various relatives, both young and old, meant there was neither the time nor money to spare.

All this changed about fifteen years ago when we recovered from nearly losing our home during an economic downturn (but that is a separate story). We found ourselves in the unexpected position of having a bit to spare and an almost empty house; with not only children having more or less flown the nest but also a reduced number of 'oldies' to consider. We decided it was now or never, and via the internet booked appointments with several *Immobiliers* (estate agents) around our favourite area of the Charente. We settled on a five day trip, hiring a car from Bergerac airport, and staying in a B&B in the centre of our search area.

We had taken to heart the lesson my parents didn't learn of never burning your bridges. On their retirement they had sold for a pittance a 100 acre farm with two houses, in order to live on a boat and cruise around the Mediterranean shores and islands. Several years later, older and less healthy, they found they could hardly afford a tiny two-bed semi back in the UK. So with this in mind we agreed to only spend what we could afford to do without, rather than over-stretching our resources, and most importantly, to keep a foothold in the 'old country'. Over many years of visiting France, we had met several ex-pats unable to return when they were older and unwell, just at the time they needed our free NHS and a doctor who spoke their language.

We also knew from experience – both ours and others – that we didn't want a huge place with lots of land; I'm allergic to housework and didn't plan to spend my time in France on cleaning, maintenance and gardening duties. Nor did we want anything that would be difficult to heat; we'd grown up in the pre-central heating, pre-double-glazing era with smelly paraffin heaters in the bathroom and single-bar electric fires which burnt your shins but left the rest of you freezing. Even in the south of France the winters can be cold.

I had grown up on a farm in England so knew that living in the middle of a farm yard would be muddy in winter and fly-infested in summer. We also knew about the French rural habit of owning guard dogs who live chained outdoors and bark at everything which passes. In French towns, front doors open right onto dusty and busy roads which didn't appeal, but nor did we want the back of beyond, all alone with miles to drive to the shops. The whole point, we agreed, was warmth, relaxation, companionship and most importantly, social interaction.

So, having done our homework and made appointments via the internet, we set off full of enthusiasm, in the certain knowledge that any one of the properties we'd arranged to view would be 'the one' and our dream would finally come true.

That February was cold. Not quite snowing but a bitter wind was blowing in from the Bay of Biscay. The first *Immobilier* near Angouleme had forgotten about us. They said the three places we'd arranged to see had already been sold, then went on to ask us how much we could spend. They showed us videos and photos of places three times the price of those we had originally booked to view. They also wanted our agreement to buy one before they would take us to actually view it.

We demurred on the grounds that, although the property might appear very pleasant in the photos, it was no good if we couldn't see the neighbouring houses and countryside. They described the prices as being 'around' or 'in the region of' which, to our English minds, was disconcerting. They did eventually agree to take us to see a property that afternoon but when we came back after lunch, the office was deserted. We decided life was too short to deal with such awkward agents, which left just five out of our original eight appointments.

A typical French village house

Our next *Immobilier* was further inland; when we arrived it was to find that office packed with noisy people, and to our dismay learned our viewings had been cancelled because the properties had been sold. We were extremely annoyed as the appointments had been confirmed just before we'd flown to Bergerac the previous day. However this time the agent agreed to drive us to three 'similar' properties, which were neither similar nor within our budget. We were beginning to sense a theme! Another wasted day, but at least we now knew what we didn't want: anything with a garden half a mile down the road, on a steep hill overlooking a factory or with a smelly oil fuel tank in the integral garage, which didn't appear to be actually connected to anything.

Driving back to the B&B we were stopped by gendarmes waving machine guns at us. Very scary. They demanded David get out of the car and open the boot, which of course he did. Fortunately we had our passports with us, and the hire documents for the car. It transpired that just a few minutes earlier a garage had been held up at gunpoint by a couple in a car similar to ours. No wonder the gendarmes wanted to check our boot for firearms. We breathed huge sighs of relief when they let us go.

Disheartened but not quite despairing, we rang the final agent with whom we had appointments scheduled for the following day. She agreed the two properties we wanted to view were still available, and that she was happy to show them to us. We therefore set off after breakfast in optimistic mood, only to be told on arrival that we really would not like the house in the Charente Maritime, we would be very disappointed in it; she would just take us to see the other one instead. We duly followed her car into the depths of the countryside; on and on we drove, becoming completely disorientated, until at last she turned up a narrow twisting farm track. There in the distance was a collection of dilapidated farm buildings surrounding a brand-new bungalow.

It transpired the old farming couple had continued to live in the ancient stone house while their son had built the modern bungalow in which he and his young family now lived. The original house, which was for sale, stood in an overgrown yard littered with bones and goat skulls. Its ancient heavy wooden door led into the dampest, most grease covered, filthy room we had ever seen, which stank of decayed food and mould. The agent quickly pointed out the amazing stone fireplace complete with original *pottager* (cooking fire) and the elegant ceiling. Our charming lady agreed the whole room would need steam cleaning whilst proudly pointing out that it did have electricity: a single fly-covered light bulb dangled from the ceiling and one socket hung precariously out of the wall. In the second ground floor room was a huge concrete vat and enormous hole in the ground where wine had been stored. Sadly it contained only a faint waft of wine long gone.

A worm-riddled door opened to disclose a steep, rotten staircase hidden inside one of the walls. Giggling nervously, (it was either that or cry) we cautiously edged our way up to the gigantic attic space. Here was treasure indeed; hundreds of ancient wine bottles (empty), original demi-johns, flagons (also unfortunately empty) and other exciting finds, including a packet of Persil and plastic baby's bath where the old lady had done her laundry. There were no windows or electricity up there but that didn't matter as daylight shone through the many holes in the roof anyway.

Outside were numerous dilapidated outhouses which had possibly housed goats as none were tall enough to stand up in. The garden was extremely overgrown and soggy.   The only source of water was from a well, rather too close to what smelt like the toilet outlet. However all this could easily be ignored for the wonderful views across a valley of open fields with woods in the distance. Just as we were admiring the old fruit trees in the orchard and the tranquility, there was a loud burst of noise as a huge tractor erupted out of the only new farm building and sped down the track leaving a cloud of smoke and dust in its wake. A tad off-putting.   Sadly, we declined this property on the grounds that it was too dilapidated and remote.

Our agent then looked at her watch and dashed off to collect her son from school!   No wonder she hadn't wanted us to view the house in the Charente Maritime. Was it us? Did we look green and stupid? or did they really not want to sell these reasonably priced places.

Thus we found ourselves abandoned in the middle of goodness knows where, with nothing else to view before catching our flight home in two days time. Wondering what to do next, we meandered north through the countryside until after about an hour of driving along narrow leafy lanes, we found a likely looking auberge which served a simple late lunch of aromatic French onion soup, succulent grey mullet on a bed of rice and velvety homemade chocolate mousse, all accompanied by a carafe of *vin ordinair* and lashings of coffee.

A delightful
Auberge

Refreshed and full of renewed optimism, we decided to ring an *Immobilier* we knew near Ruffec to see if she had anything for us to view. We had met Madam R the previous year when my brother had sold a house near this town, which he'd renovated. We'd stayed with him a few times and fallen in love with the local people and gentle landscape. The previous autumn we'd agreed to purchase a property from Madam R, once all nineteen beneficiaries who had inherited it had been found. Because they had still been searching at Christmas, we had withdrawn (ten years later it had still not been marketed). Now she said she was '*desole*' she'd not been able to progress the purchase of the house, barn and field for us; she was pleased, however, to have a couple of other places we could view the following day. This, and a slap-up evening meal in Angouleme, cheered us up no end.

TIPS AND INFORMATION

- *It's fine to use the internet to investigate prices, style of properties etc. but DO visit the area you favour. You may find it too windy, too busy, too anything, or perhaps not enough of something. If you can afford the time, even visit in different seasons.*

- *Know your intentions – will your home be for your retirement, holiday, rental, new working life etc. This will influence the size of property and amount of land you want. It's easy to be carried away by large dwellings and loads of land for a fraction of British prices, but if you're not going to live there permanently, or are already of retirement age, you have to consider how it will be maintained in the future.*

- *If you're retiring, remember with increasing age you may not want to climb stairs, paint windows, mow acres of grass, or have to drive to the shops. Don't rush to buy the first place you see; be patient.*

- *In France, holiday rentals have a very short season (six weeks from July 14th to the end of August) and clients expect all mod cons, including swimming pools, so don't expect renting out gites to be a major source of income.   Also, you will be competing against ferry companies who offer cheap crossings with their holiday homes.*

- *If you've always lived in a crowded city, an isolated house on a hilltop at the end of a track with acres of land will pull at your heart strings. However, in the winter that track will be muddy; in summer, dusty. Builders may charge extra for travel.   It's unlikely that a boulangerie will deliver and the phone/ internet could be erratic. No neighbours to talk to, or keep an eye on the property when you're not there. If you prefer your own company, splendid isolation is fine. If you are doing the work yourself, consider how often you will have to drive into town to change that packet of screws that turned out to be the wrong size...There's nothing wrong with buying 'remote' but you do need to look carefully at the practicalities.*

- *As in the UK, rural crime is on the increase in France and isolated empty properties are vulnerable. Ensure you can lock everything up safely when you aren't in residence. You will need shutters for insurance purposes.*

- *If your chosen spot is remote, check electricity and phone lines are available; that water is not only from the well. Remember as you grow older the romance of collecting buckets of water on a freezing morning or in the rain will fade. French rural phones can be spasmodic at the best of times and you'll want broadband. There is no mains gas in the countryside, it is all bottled, so electricity down-times can be a major problem.Not many rural villages have mains drainage; you will need a septic tank - 'fosse septic' or 'tout l'eau'.*

First view of our hamlet

Chapter 2

As soon as we arrived at Madam's office she bundled us into her car. We had no idea what we were about to see, but nothing could be any worse than the previous couple of days. Her poor English and our basic French, known as *Franglaise*, served us sufficiently well to enable us to understand that this property had only become available that very morning via a court order, as the sole beneficiary was a minor. We would be the first people to see it.

'You Anglaise, you 'ave no fright of *les fantomes, les spectres,*(ghosts, spirits)   *n'est pas*?' she asked us. *'Mais non, certainment pas,'* we replied, puzzled.

Five minutes later she turned off the main road towards a pretty hamlet complete with turreted *logis*, (gatehouse or lodge) a renovated *lavoir* (wash house), 12th century church, and the stone ruins of a minor chateau.   We noticed a sign pointing to *Le Cimetière* and thought Madam had been concerned that we wouldn't like being opposite the village cemetery.

This was our barn fifty years before we saw it

She drew up outside a long low stone barn set on the side of a gentle valley.   Getting out of the car, we breathed the fresh air and listened to the birds singing.

Madam informed us the French owner had begun converting the barn into a house so planning permission was already granted.   Some parts were a

16

couple of hundreds of years old. Water (cold), electricity and even a phone line were already laid on, but basically it was just a shell. The window frames were rotten and had some broken panes. The 'back' entrance was cobbled together out of packing cases while the only other door was nailed shut.

Packing case doors

A concrete floor had been laid to most rooms, with rickety block-work steps joining the top end to the lower space, a fall of about one metre.

Internal walls, made of block-work, created several rooms, some of which were open to the high roof, showing the original rough rafters. Only the kitchen and one bedroom sported ceilings, saggy and grubby. The barn was smelly, full of rubbish and very cold.

However, the roof and external walls looked sound. The 'garden' was currently a jungle of waist high weeds and not much larger than the building, which actually suited us as we didn't want too much maintenance. The external stone walls were in good condition though they didn't always meet up with the roof.

Walls should join up with roof

The asking price would leave us enough to finish the renovation. It would take a lot of work but with my background in the building trade, I knew we could make a lovely home from these bare bones. We looked at each other, wide eyed and smiling. This was more like it.

Madam R then took us to view a couple more properties. One was very small and pokey with a series of disconnected rooms which we couldn't see how to make work. David managed to put a foot through the rotten floor, releasing a cloud of mould spores into the air; I sneezed wildly. It had no garden, just a filthy overgrown yard scattered with rubbish.

The other was on a busy road with only a shallow pavement protecting the front door from the traffic. We asked if we could have a second look at the barn but Madam had other appointments. She would, however, be free at nine o'clock the following morning.

Opening onto a busy road

So we returned by ourselves to check out the village and surroundings. There was very little through traffic as the hamlet was set back from the main road. It was just a five minute drive to a small market town with post office, various shops and a *Tabac* (bar). Having helped my brother with his renovation we knew we would be frequent visitors to the nearby Commune-owned *decheterie* (rubbish tip). Additionally, the farm further down the valley was arable so no animal smells and flies.

The barn even had neighbours who could keep an eye on it in our absence. Best of all, the main structure was sound and, because it was just a shell, we thought there wouldn't be too many nasty hidden surprises. Should we buy it? It was certainly the best option we'd seen. We were definitely interested – and excited.
We spent a sleepless night of debate, brewing endless cups of tea, scribbling figures on bits of paper. We'd been looking for a couple of years and this was the most promising place we'd seen within our budget. Should we? Back and forth the conversation went into the early hours.

After a sketchy breakfast, we were on Madam's doorstep by nine o'clock, waiting as she opened the *bureau* (office). We had another very quick viewing before she led us to the *Notaire* (solicitor) to sign the preliminary papers. The *Notaire* informed us that as the sale had been ordered by the Court there was no chance of negotiating the price. We didn't care. Then it was a euphoric mad dash back to Bergerac for our afternoon flight home.

We were – or soon would be – the proud owners of an uninhabitable stone barn.   Exactly what we'd always said we didn't want. Now all we had to do was turn it into a home from home.

It shouldn't take long.   Little did we know.

TIPS AND INFORMATION

- *Any Immobilier worth his salt will have a British or fluent English-speaking agent. If they don't then ask them to repeat anything you didn't understand. Don't pretend you know what's going on if you don't. For example the French use a 24 hour clock, so it's easy to misunderstand times.   Where prices are concerned, get them to write down the figures. Ask what fees are included (the buyer pays these) and how much they are, as there is often some wiggle room on them. Hence a price being 'in the region of'.*

- *You will be asked to sign a 'l'intention d'acheter' (intent to buy) which gives you twelve days in which to change your mind, during which time you will not incur any costs should you pull out.   French purchasers are canny and tend to agree verbally to a purchase but don't sign anything for months, so they can pull out right up to the supposed completion date! But if you live in a different country, the Notaire will 'encourage' you to sign up front. This works both ways as it protects you from the owner selling to someone else in your absence.*

- *In France, the vendor has to supply survey reports on everything: electricity, plumbing, asbestos, septic tank (if there is one), termites, woodworm, bats – and anything else they can possibly think of. It is customary to not sign anything until all these are in place. You can give the Notaire – or any trusted friend who lives locally – your Power of Attorney to save you making lots of trips to and from France as signing dates tend to change at the last moment.*

- *The Notiare's fees are set in stone by the government, on a sliding scale according to the price of the property. However most Immobiliers set their fees at approximately 30% of the purchase price. Yikes, I hear you say. But these fees are negotiable. The agent tends to ask the vendor how much they want to clear from the sale (eg, 100,000 Euros). To allow room for negotiating, they will market the property for 115,000€ plus their fees so the property is advertised at 145,000€. If you offer 120,000€ the agent will negotiate with the vendor and reduce their fees accordingly so that both parties get what they want.*

Nearby chateau

Chapter 3

We tried not to bombard the Notaire for updates about progress once we'd returned home that February, but by May we were somewhat impatient and requested that the completion date be set before Bastille Day, July 14th, when the whole of France starts its summer holidays. At last Monsiuer contacted us with a date at the end of June for the final signings, money transfer and collection of keys.

We opted for a five day return ferry crossing and, trawling the internet again, I found and booked us into a nearby Chambre d'Hôte in a delightfully modernised stone house. Comfortable and offering evening meals, mine host was witty and obliging, offering plentiful wine to accompany the delicious food. The other guests were at various stages of purchase so conversation flowed easily at dinner.

Mine Host and guests at the Chamber d'hote

One couple arrived on their motor bikes; they'd already bought a plot of land and were waiting for planning permission to be granted so they could start building their *pavillon* (bungalow). Another pair arrived in a van full of furniture and ready-made bespoke kitchen units which needed to be unloaded into their already-modernised house. I'm afraid we declined to help; we had our own agenda. A third couple were just starting their search for a holiday home which had to be close enough to lively entertainment for their teenagers to enjoy.

On this trip, we needed to open a bank account so we could transfer the necessaries and organise house insurance before we completed the purchase. The bank manager was called Philippe; I'm afraid we made fun of his name and called him Monsieur Filip-Filop (behind his back naturally). The French banking system is different to ours in the UK and setting up an account is quite a lengthy process as it takes some explaining. Allow the whole morning/afternoon for your appointment and listen carefully; you might even want to make notes.

We also planned to source local contractors for *devis* (quotations) for the initial works to make the place habitable. To this end, we drove around the area, looking at recently updated houses, asking the owners for recommendations. Most were almost too friendly, inviting us in to admire their homes, regaling us with hilarious and sometimes frightening anecdotes of their experiences, and liberally supplying us with *Pineau* or other cold beverages. *Pineau* is a speciality of the Charente region, local wine fortified with Cognac. Very palatable, even at 10am. We frequently staggered back to our B&B to de-tox.

We heard of a septic tank which had been installed uphill of the house, so that when it rained hard, the tank overflowed into the property. We decided to give that builder a miss. There was the electrician who declared all the electrics needed replacing, which he then did. When his invoice came in, the owners discovered that he had installed the original 'defective' electrics. We didn't use him either. There was a couple who'd bought a house which had already been renovated. Too late they discovered that the retaining wall built on the downslope of the house didn't have any foundations. At the first sign of rain, the wall started sliding down the hillside, taking the whole back of the house with it. We hoped they'd been insured.

A few complained about contractors not turning up, or arriving too early in the morning, or starting a job on Monday and not returning until Thursday. Through further discussion, we found this was usually down to the weather. Some people had used English builders, or men purporting to be builders, who had done a shoddy job, grabbed the money and disappeared. We vowed not to use English builders.

Most though were happy customers who praised the workmanship of their contractors, but although we obtained quotations from them, in the end we didn't have to use them, as will be explained later.

At last it was time to visit the Notaire who handed us the keys to our own little piece of France. That evening we shared a bottle or two of bubbly with our fellow guests over dinner. Breakfast was a rather quiet affair the next morning as we nursed tender heads, after which our new friends followed us to the barn, eager to view our purchase.

Not all of them were impressed! To be brutally honest, none of them were, and to be fair it was very smelly. They saw a scruffy barn not a house; whereas we saw a skeleton which had nothing to hide; they didn't have our vision. We had chosen to buy a really cheap property so we had enough money to pay for professionals to install the septic tank, the plumbing and the electrics. I had experience of building projects having worked for a structural engineer and an architect, so understood how to project manage. To us, the main structure was sound, the work was mostly cosmetic; we were looking forward to the challenge.

The French idea of clearing out a property is different to ours. The vendor may even leave stuff in a locked shed to be collected 'later'. Later can be several years hence and in French law if you know they want it, you are not allowed to use, sell or throw it away. Best to check whether the property has been cleared while you have a translator at the Notaire's office. Better still, don't take the vendor's word for it; make a quick visit to the property before your appointment. (We hadn't).

TIPS AND INFORMATION

- *French banking is more complex than in the UK. Once you have written out a cheque it is legal tender and cannot be cancelled. The banks charge for providing a bank card. They can arrange property insurance but make sure it is correct for you. For example, if you buy a stone house, you need a 'like for like' policy otherwise any rebuilding will be in cheaper modern materials. Also ensure the insurance covers the property being left empty for long periods of time. Allow a couple of hours for your appointment, and possibly take a French/English dictionary with you.*

- *Allow the whole morning (or afternoon) for your completion appointment with the Notaire. The vendor will also attend and each page of the contract document will be read out by the Notaire. Both the purchaser and the vendor then initial each page, with the words 'lu et approuve' (read and approved). You can have a translator – often your bi-lingual Immobilier – who will explain your responsibilities and those of the Vendor. This all takes time and the Notaire will not be rushed.*

- *British banks offer a range of accounts, some of which offer commission-free exchange rates when you use their credit card abroad. Some offer personal travel insurance for a small monthly fee. It is worth researching which will be best for you. We used Nationwide but other banks have accounts with offers which may suit you better.*

- *Also research financial institutions who will allow you to transfer large sums of money abroad at a better rate of exchange than a high street bank. We used HIFEX but deals change all the time, so shop around.*

- *While we're on the subject of finance, check your car insurance for travel/breakdown abroad.*

Rubbish left in the garage

CHAPTER 4

Our first visit to OUR French property was marred only by the mess and filthy rubbish that had not been cleared out. We now realise this is normal in France, but at the time we were horrified to say the least. However our Guardian Angel was looking after us and as we stood knee deep in nettles, thistles and general detritus, wondering where to start, an English voice greeted us from the road.

'Hello, I noticed the English number plates on your car. You must be my new neighbours,'

'Oh, hi. Yes, we've just completed today.' We were delighted to have an English neighbour, whose knowledge of the area would be helpful.

'I'm Anna; I live just over there,' she said pointing to the house on the other side of the road. 'I know you'll be busy but please do come over for a chat. I might even run to an aperitif.'

There wasn't a lot we could do in the barn. We hadn't expected it to be full of rubbish so we didn't have gloves or cleaning equipment with us. We took a few photographs, then after trying to pile some of the mess out of the way, we decided to take up Anna's kind offer.

Having run the gauntlet of her very friendly collie, we sat at Anna's kitchen table and exchanged histories. Anna had lived in France for several years, running a bed and breakfast nearby before buying in this hamlet just the year before; so she had known the previous owner of our barn.

'Mnsr. J. moved his lady friend and baby son in about three years ago, and started to turn the barn into a house while they lived in it. But he kept running out of money and the girl wasn't much help.' Anna told us. 'They were very poor and she obviously couldn't cope with his moods and the basic conditions. She moved out, taking the little boy with her. Mnsr. J. became depressed, working less and less; then tried to commit suicide a couple of times. Yoyo (another neighbour) and I found him one day inside the *armoire* (wardrobe) sobbing his heart out. He finally hanged himself from one of the rafters about eight months ago. We had to call the *gendarmes* (police) to cut him down. It wasn't very nice.'

I gasped, enthralled, but David, being more prosaic, said, 'Well at least with the cemetery just across the road he didn't have far to go for his final resting place.' This comment was perhaps a bit short on empathy, as our new friend looked rather shocked.

We had heard some of this from Madam R, but Anna relished telling us in greater detail. She suggested we have the barn blessed by a priest before moving in, to make sure his spirit was not lingering. No wonder Madam R had asked if we were afraid of ghosts. More to appease Anna than because I felt it was necessary, I agreed to say prayers and sprinkle holy water. I did sing the 23rd Psalm but my holy water was anti-bacterial spray.

Anna had worked for an *Immobilier* for a while and knew the local builders and their phone numbers. She promised to ring around and arrange for various artisans to meet us next time we visited.

'You need a mason to install the *fosse septic* or *tout l'eau* (septic tank system), a plumber for internal pipework and a carpenter for pretty much everything else,' she explained as we exchanged details. We promised to let her know in good time what date we would arrive in September. Breathing a sigh of relief at our good fortune, we left a key with her.

We spent the summer at home collecting furniture and tools, then September found us back in our friendly *Chambre d'Hote*. Anna summoned the contractors and acted as translator on this first meeting. They weren't impressed by the smell and trash in the house but we promised it would be clean and empty before they started work.

The original
bathroom -
17' x 11'

The plumber agreed to send us a *devis* (quotation) for bathroom, toilet and kitchen plumbing and to provide catalogues of the necessary fittings.

The mason – a dumpy little man who resembled Pooh bear and sported a wandering eye – agreed to quote for installing the *tout l'eau*; rural France rarely runs to mains drainage. He would also concrete the earthen floor in the garage, add ridge tiles as necessary to the roof and finish the outer stone wall so that it joined up to the roof – a useful feature to have in a house. There was a finial on one gable end which Mnsr le Mason informed us was *ancien* (vintage) and would be impossible to match. I had already bought a weather vane sporting a cockerel, the Charentaise symbol, which he agreed would be a good alternative on the other gable.

Mason finishing the stone wall

The carpenter undertook to make double glazed external doors and windows, install ceilings where necessary, fit waterproof *placoplâtre* (plaster-board) to the breeze-block bathroom walls, and, most importantly, act as Site Manager, co-ordinating the various trades.

It transpired that we could not have chosen better people. They were used to working together and, being of a 'certain maturity' had old fashioned ethics about workmanship. Our carpenter was a perfectionist as well as an artisan and carefully crafted an English style stable door to our specification. Although in all other ways he helped us to retain the Charentaise look to our renovations, our Main Man, as he became, was so taken with our design that he offered it to his other clients. We quickly learned to trust his judgement and listen to his advice.

More rubbish left in the loft

We spent the rest of our visit emptying and cleaning the barn. Donning heavyweight gloves, we began to clear the loft of smelly bits of old carpets, soggy cardboard and other items that had been used as insulation. Once these had been thrown down into the garage area, we stuffed them into plastic sacks ready for transport. Mnsr J. had left clothes, toys and broken furniture as well as lots of what can only be described as unpleasant rubbish, all of which were carted to the *decheterie* (local tip) which fortunately was only a ten minute drive away.

The *decheterie* is where you can take everything from garden cuttings to batteries, glass and other general rubbish. Each commune or group of villages has one and they are free to everyone in that commune. But NEVER try to use one outside your commune. Until the *Chef de Decheterie* (Tip Manager) knows your vehicle by sight, he will ask for your address.

Faced with such a daunting amount of mess, we were delighted when some Dutch friends, who had a holiday home nearby, offered the use of their trailer to help with this mammoth task. We counted ourselves very lucky that we already knew a few people from our visits to my brother's house in a nearby village. Even using their van and trailer, it took eight trips to the *decheterie* over two days before we had space in the barn to move around.

One load heading to the decheterie

To repay their generosity, we treated them to a slap up meal at the nearby 'posh' restaurant, *Le Cheval Blanc*, where the other diners were smartly dressed and dripping with jewellery. We had showered, but our evening attire was definitely workmanlike.

Because we didn't have a good signal for our mobile phones, we were grateful that initially Anna used her landline to talk to utilities and contractors on our behalf. In this way we contacted *Emmaus* (the national charity warehouse) to take away anything useful that we didn't want. Then we swept and cleaned with anti-bacterial spray the now empty rooms. At this stage, we were especially grateful to Mine Host and his wife who supplied us with sandwiches for lunch and provided hot showers and suppers on our return each evening. As we were still at the 'bucket and chuck-it' stage of plumbing and had nowhere to cook, their generous facilities were doubly welcome.

A degree of ingenuity was required to rid the barn of some of the rubbish. Two full commodes really taxed our imagination (no, I'm not telling you where we deposited them); old tyres found a new home joining others already holding down a tarpaulin on a nearby hayrick; and an open tray of car oil had to be carefully poured into a proper container before it could be transported to the *decheterie*.

Clothes, batteries, broken furniture, rusty tools and fishing trophies were bagged for removal. An old, worm-infested piano was chopped up as it was too heavy to manoeuvre; and we held our noses as we dragged out several sodden mattresses. Don't even ask why they were soaking.

The 'toilet', complete with full commodes.

By the time we had to return to the UK the barn was empty, clean and ready for the workmen to begin.

Needless to say, they didn't.

TIPS AND INFORMATION

- *Before signing the completion documents at the Notaire's office, do have a quick look around the property to make sure it is empty. We didn't and were left with a lot of rubbish to dispose of before we could even begin to renovate.*

- *Do provide yourself with gloves; gardening style as well as latex ones, for cleaning and handling heavy items.*

One of our new neighbours
Chapter 5

Read your *devis* or quotation very carefully, if necessary with the aid of a dictionary. Once you have signed and returned it, you are locked into that contractor, even if he keeps you waiting a year or more. Therefore insist it includes either an estimated date of commencement or a 'get out' clause whereby you can go elsewhere if he hasn't started within, say, six months.

Always get quotations from more than one artisan but don't necessarily pick the cheapest; take into account how long he plans to take on the job and whether he is a registered SIRET company (with a government issued number, proving the company is bona fide). Any builder worth his salt will be busy so expect to wait before he can start on your job.

One advantage of the French system is that, when you employ a properly SIRET registered French builder, his costs can be added to the purchase price. So keep your invoices to defray against Capital Gains Tax for when you or your beneficiaries sell the property. It is important to keep all paperwork as you may also need to prove that such things as electrics and plumbing have been done in accordance with current standards.

The mason does all the stonework, the external plumbing and concrete floor slabs. The plumber fits internal pipework, chimney and guttering. The carpenter fixes plasterboard, kitchen, doors etc. None of them will cross the line into the others' trades. Thus the mason will only take *fosse* pipes to the house wall, and then the plumber has to join them to his internal runs.

Draw up a budget; the purchase price includes the agents and Notaire fees. Factor in ferry costs, travel expenses which might include toll fees if you use the wonderful French autoroutes and possibly an overnight stay in a B&B if your purchase isn't close to the ferry port. When you calculate the cost of doing up your property, remember all those 'extras' which no one ever mentions. For example, your tiles are priced per square metre, but the tile adhesive and grouting will double this cost. Screws, rawl plugs, light fittings etc all mount up alarmingly. Even if the property is already modernised you will probably want to change or update things to your own taste.

Some items are best bought in UK (paint for example). Most French towns have a 3MMM or Mr Bricolage (DIY stores) but they aren't cheap. If you can, wait for their sales to buy such things as insulation (*isolation*), wiring, ladders, tiles etc.

Allow a contingency sum. Then double it.

I have merely 'O' level French but having visited France many times had acquired some confidence in being able to string together simple sentences and, almost more importantly, to understand the answers. David didn't know any French so invested in a Hugo course 'Learn French in three months'. Ten years later he is still on the first chapter! However he read a French dictionary every night to learn building terms. So with my knowledge of grammar and his vocabulary, we just about got by. Anna was a godsend at the beginning as she gave us confidence that we and our contractors understood each other. We bought a French Business Dictionary as well as the Shorter French Dictionary, both published by Harrap. Hefty tomes but well worth having.

Because our barn was in a valley, and had thick stone walls, initially our mobiles only worked if we held them above the fridge. Why this spot caught a signal we never knew but we took to keeping our phones on top of the fridge and would stand close to it while talking to friends or contractors.

Double-glazed French doors replaced the packing case doors.

TIPS AND INFORMATION

- *Mobile phone coverage has improved, even in rural areas, but make sure you have international calls in your contract.*

- *A good dictionary is a must. The French Business Dictionary and the Shorter French Dictionary, both published by Harrap, give a wide vocabulary, including colloquialisms.*

February in the Charente
Chapter 6

We Brits don't expect French winters to be as cold as the UK, but they are. The winter season is shorter, but sub-zero temperatures in the Charente, and indeed in the south, are not unusual. One of the hardest things to do, if you're not used to advance planning, is deciding whether you want central heating before the plumbing is installed and floors laid. Fitting radiators and pipes can be very difficult in stone houses unless there is no floor screed or it needs replacing, when underfloor heating can be installed relatively easily. Our floors were already concreted and a couple of rooms had tile or laminate flooring already laid, and anyway our budget didn't stretch to central heating, so we knew we would need electric radiators instead.

Naturally work didn't start in our absence, let alone progress. E-mails back and forth between us and our neighbour Anna mentioned our disappointment –– already a year had passed since we had agreed to buy and we were no nearer having a habitable house. Some of the excuses were valid, others laughable. The contractors had other jobs lined up, the weather wasn't suitable, the ground was too hard for Mnsr le Mason to install the *fosse* so Mnsr le Plombier could not start and Mnsr le Charpentier was still making the windows and doors, ready to install in the spring. And anyway, we weren't there to make decisions, or pay their invoices!

The JCB digging the hole for the
concrete septic tank

One dismal, UK February evening, the phone rang just as we arrived home from work. It was Anna, informing us that a JCB was in our garden digging a huge hole. She agreed to send photos via e-mail. I made a quick call to the Chambre d'Hote, then we booked a couple of days off work and a five day ferry special to dash out to see for ourselves. Our excitement knew no bounds as we watched the septic tank being installed and took pictures of the array of pipes going hither and thither.

The sand filtration bed in front of the tank

Mnsr le Mason, whom we had nick-named Pooh Bear – he had the same shape as that well known bear – was cross-eyed so we never knew which eye to look at when talking to him. We were concerned that he wouldn't cope if he had to climb ladders as, while one eye was fixed, the other roved. Once the JCB had dug the large hole for the tank it left in a cloud of smoke, its wheels throwing mud high into the air. Then a van and trailer arrived with a mini digger to gouge out a trench for the pipes to the house.

Our hearts were in our mouths when Mnsr le Mason attempted to reverse it from the trailer and drive it down our sloping garden. First he fell off the ramp when the digger was half way down, and then he managed to tip the whole thing on its side once in the garden. He tried to reverse himself out of the cab, bottom first. But he got stuck. David and I retreated into the house, peeping through the window trying to muffle our giggles while his workforce helped him. One held up his trousers (his braces had given up the ghost) while the other chap grabbed him around the waist and tugged. Once freed he stalked off and got into his van. We worried that he might meet cars on the road, but his son reassured us. The van was well known and local drivers gave him a wide berth.

Anna had rung Mnsr le Plombier to advise him of our unexpected arrival so he met us with the promised catalogues. He drew proposed positions for the bathroom furniture in chalk on the concrete floor. We agreed on toilet, hand basin, bidet, shower tray and taps. We took his advice on the position of the hot water tank and agreed he should add plumbing for a washing machine to the quote. We asked him to take the pipes up to the first floor as we planned to put a bathroom and a couple of bedrooms upstairs in Phase Two.

Things were moving.   At last.

Imagine our shock when *Mnsr le Marie* (the Mayor), who up until then had been very helpful, came along and stopped the external work! Apparently our *devis* had been for an 'old style' fosse – that is, for a simple septic tank. New government legislation was insisting on an electric pump to take any waste water from a sand filtration bed up to the drain in the road. Unfortunately the mason couldn't give us a *devis* for the extra work until after we'd gone home, but as it was a legal requirement we agreed to authorise it anyway. We later learned that Mnsr le Maire made it his business to 'vet' the new *devis* and adjust it downwards on our behalf, so although the cost increased, it didn't double. He also oversaw the work in our absence which was reassuring.

During this impromptu visit we started removing the *lambris* (wooden slats – very popular cheap finish in old houses) from the bathroom and kitchen walls – they were dark, damp and smelly, so had to go. Some of the walls had black motifs stencilled on them and a couple of beams in a bedroom had been painted dark blue, so I sealed in the colour with my trusty PVA glue (one part PVA, five parts water) before painting them white. Choosing the least smelly bedroom, I opened a 5 litre can of magnolia and began the task of making it habitable. Unfortunately it was even colder inside than out – minus 13 degrees – and not really suitable for painting so I didn't get far. Almost before we knew it our five days were up and it was time to go home again.

Anna continued to keep us informed via e-mail: 'the fosse has gone in; the garden's a mess; he's relaid the path; the plumber has installed the bath, bidet and handbasin; internal pipes are connected to the fosse; the new double-glazed windows and doors look fabulous; I have the new keys to give you.'

New windows and doors - no shutters yet.

'It took one and a half lorry loads of ready mix cement to lay the floor in the garage. The lorries blocked the road for most of the day but no one complained, they just took the opportunity to have a nose around. There's *plaquo* (slang for plaster-board) on the bathroom walls and ceiling.' Anna kept us in a perpetual state of excitement for which we were grateful. We couldn't wait until we were able to visit again.

Our road was very quiet. On the outskirts of the hamlet, we were one of only five houses. As well as Anna, opposite her and to our west were an elderly French couple, the other side of them was an English couple who had bought just before us, and to our east was a sprightly French man. The very quiet 'residents' in the village cemetery opposite completed our immediate neighbours. Some of our new acquaintances at the B&B had asked if we weren't bothered about being so close to the cemetery, but we reassured them that, apart from on Halloween, we reckoned they wouldn't cause us any trouble.

Pierrot and Yoyo (our immediate French neighbours) were delighted to see the barn being occupied; they had been most upset by Mnsr J's suicide, especially as Yoyo had been the one to find him.

Anna's house in the foreground,
Yoyo's next to her,
Andre's garden and house behind the barn.

Pierrot had lived next door all his life; he had brought Yoyo there on their marriage. They lived on fruit and vegetables which they grew in their one acre plot; with chickens and rabbits for eggs and meat and, apart from bread, were mostly self-sufficient. They were incredibly difficult to understand as they spoke the local patois at full speed, but were very friendly and kept giving me plants for our garden; a bit premature as it was currently an overgrown mass of weeds.

Talking to them made me feel like the *gendarme* in 'Ello 'ello, who gets his pronunciation hilariously wrong. Yoyo would jabber away at me and I just had to smile and nod, hoping I shouldn't be frowning and shaking my head. She introduced me to the bread delivery van which visited at the same time twice a week. If any of us were going to miss Bernadette's arrival, which she signalled by a long blast on the van horn, we would hang a bag and money for the order on Yoyo's gate.

Our other English neighbours had retired from the Army, and so were used to being posted all over the world. They spoke even less French than us, and preferred to make friends among the ex-pat English community rather than mingling with the locals. They were very hospitable and over the years we spent many a liquid evening – and indeed lunches – in each other's company.

TIPS AND INFORMATION

• *Your contractors will not do much (any) work while you aren't on site. Firstly because you aren't there to shout at them so they'll go and work for someone who is. Secondly they won't want to complete the job only to find you don't like it or have changed your mind. Third, they need you on site to inspect the work and pay them.   The good contractor will not expect an 'up front' payment but will want to be paid promptly, possibly in increments if the work is over a period of time.   Don't give the Brits a bad name by delaying this.*

· *Builders are builders the whole world over. Some are good, others not so. A good contractor will be busy so don't expect him to start work as soon as you've signed the devis. Also remember that clients are the same the world over; some listen to advice before making a decision, others change their minds halfway through the project or are downright unreasonable. Make sure you are in the former group; your contractors will go the extra mile once they trust you.*

· *Your commune Mayor wields a lot of power, but some aren't sympathetic to the Brits. Best to keep on their good side, discuss external changes to the property in advance; possibly find a suitable 'incentive' to gain their cooperation; ours liked English style rich fruit cake. Bribery? Never.*

· *The Screwfix catalogue makes excellent bed-time reading; it offers a wide range of items you will need at reasonable prices.   In fact it will become your Bible.*

· *Never throw anything away.   That old dustbin lid becomes an ideal cement mixing tray; trestles can be made from odd bits of wood; bend a piece of wire into a useful temporary hook.*

- *Lists will be your friend. Make a list of the tools and equipment you leave so you don't duplicate on the next visit. Write lists of things you need to take to France, the things you are taking back, clothes you are leaving. Otherwise that one screwdriver or can of silicone will always be in the other house!*

- *Keep a notebook for meter readings, measurements, sizes, in your handbag/car at all times, both home and away. Measure everything – several times – otherwise that one piece of information you need, you won't have.*

Made it. Horse trailer loaded with furniture

Chapter 7

Just one year on from our first sight of the barn, Spring
Bank holiday coincided with the barn being secure
enough for us to take furniture and utensils. We
packed my horse trailer (well scrubbed out) with things
I'd kept from my parents' house, as well as second
hand furniture and fittings we'd acquired over the last
year: bedding and towels, spare crockery and
saucepans, bikes, mattresses and wooden bed frames,
Mum's fridge freezer and microwave. The springs
groaned with the weight. How David fitted it all in I
don't know.

At that time David was managing a furniture store and if items were already damaged when they arrived in the shop, they were often just thrown into the skip. He happily retrieved broken tables and battered chairs to repair. In this way we acquired a round kitchen table with a black top and white pedestal leg; a dozen chairs with wonky legs from which he fashioned six complete ones, and a couple of comfy easy chairs. These were all loaded into the trailer.

We had invited my architect boss and his wife to accompany us so James could make a proper survey of the barn. At the last moment David was unable to take time out from work, and James' wife also cried off, so my boss and I set off with my son Hal as 'chaperone'. The Customs officers gave us some funny looks and comments; they were concerned that we had undeclared animals with us. A quick look inside the trailer persuaded them there wasn't even room for a mouse.

James had offered to do a thorough survey of the barn in case there were any major faults which needed repair. David wanted to fashion a third bedroom and hoped that James would see a cheap way to make this possible. Having a professional set of drawings to give to our contractors made   it easier for them to place such things as electrical and bathroom fittings.

We had a meal on board the ferry which saved time on the French drive. From Dieppe we drove via Rouen then west until we met the A38 which passes Le Mans and Tours. At Poitiers we joined the RN10 (Route National) as far as Ruffec. As I was used to towing I did most of the driving while James aimed his camera out of the window and Hal dozed in the back.

It was a slow journey; my aged 4 x 4 unable to reach much above 45mph most of the time with the suspension complaining over every bump, but at last we arrived. First things first, the camping gas and kettle. While James took measurements, photographs and notes, Hal and I unloaded the trailer. Thankfully we had a sack trolley with us so were able to manoeuvre the washing machine without too much trouble. Then Hal made up one of the beds – by which I mean screwed together the wooden frame. The second bed would have to wait in bits until the other bedroom was painted.

We knew from my parents' life on board a boat that ventilation is the key to keeping damp at bay when the house is closed up, so we had carefully chosen wooden beds with legs rather than divans, and we made sure the easy chairs also had wooden legs leaving space between the floors and upholstery.

Wooden bed in newly painted bedroom

At last everything was inside; the kitchen and bedroom were crowded with enough furniture for four rooms, the bikes were in the newly concreted garage. Our barn was beginning to look almost habitable.

Original kitchen with reclaimed
table and chairs

Still without a toilet or safe electrics, we stayed with our English neighbours on this occasion. To mark our appreciation of their hospitality, we treated them and Anna to a meal in a nearby restaurant before waving au revoir once more.

A convivial meal with the neighbours

By this time we knew to the minute how long the drive should take, as well as the best places for lunch and toilet stops. But despite allowing an extra hour with the now-empty trailer our journey home was both slow yet more exciting. To cheers all round, my old 4 x 4 managed to overtake a lorry on the autoroute. Sadly we were then held up for ages by an overturned wide-load lorry which blocked both carriageways.

We sat in the resulting traffic jam impatiently watching the minutes tick by. Eventually, desperate to avoid missing our ferry, I inched into the outside lane and U turned, trailer and all, out of the queue, up onto the grass central reservation and across to the other side of the dual carriageway; then we searched for an alternative route north. Please note this is NOT advisable, probably not even legal, but there was no oncoming traffic as both sides of the road were blocked. On checking the rear view mirror, we realised we'd started a trend as a stream of cars followed us. We caught the ferry by the skin of our teeth; we were last aboard and had the dubious honour of feeling the ramp rise beneath us as we drove onto the boat.

Heading home on the Autoroute

TIPS AND INFORMATION

- *You will need a suitable vehicle to carry your tools and furniture, and reliable enough to eat up the many miles you will travel. We chose a Citroen C3 hatchback, whose interior capacity and suspension even coped with the wood-burner stove.*

- *One of our best buys from Screwfix was an industrial Henry vacuum cleaner which coped with water as well as grit, dust etc.*

- *We had thought the usual two week holidays twice a year, would be sufficient to do the renovation, but quickly realised that not only was two weeks a bit tight for finishing jobs, but we discovered we both wanted and needed to visit more frequently. We therefore booked one week off work at Easter, then another two or three weeks at the end of May, followed by as long as we could in September. Later, David took early retirement so was able to visit on his own – which we both enjoyed !*

- *Screws, rawl plugs, etc. are cheaper in England. Unless money is no object, you will find yourself spending as long in Homebase and B & Q as in 3MMM or Mr Bricolage, comparing prices.*

A working toilet - no more buckets!
Chapter 8

Our next visit, at the end of May, found a toilet installed in the tiny windowless room we had nicknamed The Dungeon. Yippee! No more buckets. At last we could stay in our barn.

This small room still had rough walls and no ceiling, but the door opened and closed, even though it didn't have a handle. Mnsr le Plombier had also installed the bath, bidet, hand basin and shower tray in the main bathroom. However he couldn't fit the toilet or the shower taps until the floor and walls had been tiled in the appropriate places. So, armed with a book on tiling, David knelt as in prayer, trying to decide where the tiles should go. His problem was that the book said you should start from the middle of the room. We didn't have time for him to do this as our bathroom was 17 feet long and 11 feet wide and we only had two days left before my brother and his wife were due to stay.

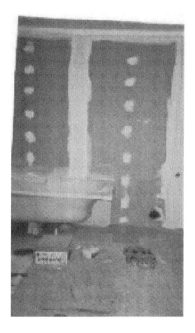

Where to start the tiling?

Many chalk lines were drawn, the laser measure was used repeatedly; finally he decided to compromise by only tiling the square foot of floor below the actual toilet and the wall behind it; also the shower wall where the tap would be fitted. With the adhesive finally mixed, he took a deep breath and …got it right first go.

A slow start but a proper job. His tiling had a really professional finish of which we were both very proud . Being a big room, we were grateful that we'd found tiles reduced in a sale; they looked fabulous and gave the bathroom a real 'wow' factor.

As I've mentioned, our bathroom was particularly large. So we had to ensure the furniture fitted it. Although the bath was normal size, we chose a large hand basin and shower tray and had plenty of room for a bidet too; particularly useful for cutting down on the amount of toilet paper going into the septic tank. However the separate loo was a very narrow room so we chose a shallow rectangular hand basin rather than a curved one.

David had never done much DIY; his first idea has always been to call in a man. He knew how to use a screwdriver, but he'd always refused to have tools bought for presents on the grounds that he might have to use them. His motto is 'If it's not perfect, it's not finished'; whereas mine is 'Finished is better than perfect.' Thus, when he does something, it's done properly. This means, as with the tiling, he takes a long time to think things through before starting the job in hand.

Because we intended to leave the property unoccupied, especially in the winter, we asked the plumber to fit a drain tap under the hot water tank so it could be emptied before we left.

Bathroom - tiled

Burst pipes are a major problem for modernised houses because they've only recently had indoor plumbing and most don't have any insulation.

Neat pipes under
the tank.

New tank with
washing machine
in front

On the advice of our plumber our hot water tank was
placed on the wall in the centre of the house, close to
the kitchen so there wasn't too long a run to any taps.
'If it's in the loft or against an outer wall,' he said, (but in
French), 'it could be prone to freezing in the winter.'
However as the cloakroom was some 40 feet from the
bathroom, the run would be so long it wasn't worth
plumbing hot water to it. Instead we installed a small
electric immersion heater.

At the same time, we asked the plumber to extend hot,
cold and outflow pipes up to the roof space before the
walls were covered in plaster-board, so installing a

bathroom upstairs at a later date would not disturb the already finished ground floor. If you do this, make sure the pipes are capped so smells don't leak out, and nothing falls in.

Pipes from bathroom, with extensions
(far corner going up to loft)

While David tiled the bathroom I carried on painting the toilet and second bedroom, ready for my brother Brett's arrival to help with the electrics.

The finished toilet and
hand basin

When we'd stayed at the house Brett was renovating, we had noticed that the village church rang the bells every half an hour from seven in the morning until seven at night. However at 7am it would ring something like fifty times, to wake the labourers from their slumber. At noon it would then ring another fifty times so that the field workers knew it was lunch time, and then at seven in the evening it would go mad again, clanging away so everyone knew it was time to go to bed.

This tradition was extremely useful in the days before the peasants owned watches or clocks. However in our hamlet we were surprised to find that not only did the church continue this practice – although it was now electronically controlled – but it surpassed other churches by ringing some seventy times in the morning, another eighty-four times at noon and again seventy in the evening. At lunchtime, 12.30 until 1.30, there was only one peel every half an hour, which could be muddling. We ended up saying to each other 'It's bong o'clock.'

Anna's collie dog either hated or loved (no one knew which) the bells and she would howl – or sing – every time they rang. We used to pray for a southerly wind, especially in the morning.

As we were now staying in our own house and the weather was gorgeous, on this visit we met most of the villagers on our evening walks. There were twenty-five properties in our hamlet, several of which were unoccupied and in various stages of disrepair, such as the one pictured in Chapter 17.

Our other immediate French neighbour, Andre, lived alone in his home since his wife had gone into care. He had dealt in antiques and was knowledgeable on many subjects. We became good friends but the locals didn't really get on with him; the rural community is quite introverted, and they tend to mistrust 'outsiders', especially those from Paris. Andre had
the added disadvantage of having a rather abrupt manner. As a result he found the English more congenial.

One young couple had lived in Paris before moving to the country when the man had suffered burnout from his rock 'n' roll lifestyle. They were doing up a wreck of a house and spoke some English so with our fractured French, we enjoyed several lively evenings together.

The *Logis* was owned by an internationally renowned sculptor whose wife and children stayed in the village while he travelled the world. He had an *atelier* (workshop) in a nearby town where he also displayed his finished work.

A work in progress outside the *Logis*

Another young French family lived in the barely habitable mini chateau. Franc showed us around, pointing out the arrow slit windows, the unsafe spiral staircase in the turret, the roof open to the sky... He, his wife and two children lived in the kitchen; they had a four-poster bed in one corner where they all slept. And we thought we'd taken on a challenge!

There were two English couples on the other side of our valley; one only visited during the school holidays so we rarely saw them as we tended to visit in May/ June and again in September. The second pair were rather disgruntled with us; they had been hoping to buy the barn for their daughter, but hadn't registered their interest with Madam R. So when we turned up on the day the Notaire received permission to sell it we were the first (and last) to view the property. They hadn't liked being piped to the post. They did thaw towards us eventually.

We got to know Yoyo and Pierrot better on this trip. Yoyo had a weekly slot on Radio Angouleme talking about the history of the Charente and its *patois*. Pierrot liked to make use of the communal water for his vegetable plot. Apparently it is law that every village makes *potable* (drinkable) water available to everyone, from the richest to the poorest.

So there is a tap outside the *Hotel de Maire* (Mayor's office) for use by everyone, free of charge. Pierrot would drive his rotovator passed our house, at two miles an hour, to the square, towing his home made trailer with a huge metal barrel and a couple of milk churns. We used to chuckle and say, 'There goes the local chapter of the Hell's Angels'.

Pierrot with his
rotovator

As well as working hard all day, we enjoyed several convivial evenings in Anna's and other neighbours' gardens, with tables laden with snacks and drink. On the rare evenings we dined alone we sat on our terrace, star gazing and watching bats and owls flitting above our heads. Bliss.

Roll on September and our next stay in our second home.

TIPS AND INFORMATION

- *English plumbing doesn't fit the French systems. The water pressure is much higher than in the UK, so don't buy taps in England to use in France - and vice versa.*

- *Insulate your loft space. That's where most heat goes. The local DIY centers (in the Charente 3MMM and Mr. Bricolage abound) have offers every year on 'isolation'. You should wear gloves, protective clothing and a mask to avoid breathing in harmful fibreglass dust while handling it.*

- *Old French buildings do not have damp proof courses or membranes and the walls, though thick, are single skin. The answer to dry interiors is ventilation and insulation. Plaster-board is fixed to a metal framework which leaves a gap between it and the wall for ventilation. Plaster-board can be bought with or without insulation, while that suitable for damp places (ie, bathrooms) is treated with a damp-resistant substance and coloured green. It still needs to be covered with tiles where it will be splashed. A gap should be left between the bottom of the plaster-board and floor, to stop any damp from rising up the wall.*

• *Plaster-board soaks up paint like an alcoholic downs whisky. Use thinned down PVA to seal it before applying paint. UK paint is cheaper and better quality than the French. Depending on how large an area needs painting, think about using one colour initially to save washing out rollers and brushes all the time. When you've finished painting for the day, wrap the roller and brush in a plastic bag or cling film, then place them and the paint tray in a plastic carrier bag, wrapping it tightly to keep the air out; this will stop paint drying hard. Make sure you shut the paint tin lid properly.*

The 12th Century church
Chapter 9

My brother had already renovated a house in the
Charente and was currently in the process of
overseeing and finishing a new build in the south of
France. To cut costs he had undertaken a French

electrical course (the French system is, naturally, different from the UK), so he agreed to give us a week of his time to upgrade the dangerous electrics installed by the previous owner. The existing lights and sockets led directly from the mains without bothering with a fuse box. Some of the electrics were merely bare wires wrapped in nylon stockings or thin cloth.

The 'loft' was little more than a huge, unfloored, roof space, criss-crossed by beams and low rafters, so we had to be very careful where we walked. The long-time home to mice, spiders and birds of all sizes, it was dusty, smelly and very hot. Brett, with David as Chief Mate, began to make sense of all the scraps of wiring strewn around between the beams.   They scrabbled around in the roof space for most of the week, drilled holes in walls for light switches and electrical sockets, and led new wires behind the plaster-board walls. My sister-in-law Carol and I threaded thin blue, red and yellow wires through thick plastic sleeves called '*gains*'. When our services were not required by the electricians, I steamed off ugly wallpaper prior to painting, while Carol looked after the food side of things, as well as running errands and shopping for supplies. She even made a start on clearing nettles and docks from the garden.

Wires straight from the
meter box

In order to chase the new wiring into the kitchen walls, David started cutting into the breeze block inner wall with his electric drill. This meant I had to stop painting and act as Mate for Brett in the loft.   It had been probably the hottest week of the year, and working in the roof space was like being in a sauna. We had to balance precariously on the joists, moving sheets of plywood to sit on as we changed positions. Brother / sister relations became somewhat strained until at last, with his head at an awkward angle and his arm shaking with the effort of holding wires aloft to fix to a rafter, Brett asked me to fetch a screwdriver from the tool box. I returned with careful steps along a beam, only to have him snap 'no, the OTHER one' which sent me scuttling back along the beam.

It's surprising how time seems to stop when the unexpected happens. As my foot missed the beam and punched a hole through the *lambris* ceiling, I flung out my arms to grab a joist. My unorthodox arrival into the kitchen somewhat startled Carol, who dropped lunch with a scream. David had been drilling holes in the wall below and did not appreciate bits of wood and plaster raining down on him. They looked up to see my legs and lower half (ok, bottom) dangling through the hole. Not a pretty sight. Brett dropped the wires he'd been holding, and both men shouted 'don't move,' at the same time. A rather superfluous instruction, I felt, as (*a*) I couldn't if I had wanted to, and (*b*) I didn't want to.

David fetched a chair to stand on and with Brett pulling from above, started feeding me back up through the hole in the ceiling. Dignified it was not. It felt as though it took forever as the men kept collapsing with laughter and Carol was crying hysterically. At last I managed to hook one leg over a beam and finally wriggled my way up into the loft again, whereupon we all paused to gather our breath.

This incident left us rather shaken so we downed tools and indulged in an early lunch, treating ourselves to a couple of beers each. I was very lucky, only suffering some nasty bruises on my *derrière*, which had taken the brunt of hitting the joists and beam. For the rest of the day I was accused of sense of humour failure as the others kept sniggering to themselves. Years later, my backside still retains the beam-shaped-dent.

The lambris ceiling
in the kitchen

David spent the rest of the afternoon patching the hole, but we all agreed the *lambris* ceiling was not a thing of beauty, being dark brown and having many gaps through which insects and dust could fall.   We eventually replaced it with plaster-board.

To add injury to insult (the insult being everyone's inability to stop laughing for the rest of the week), Carol decided she fancied a long walk that evening.   The men refused to move from their easy chairs so reluctantly I agreed to accompany her. She wanted to visit some friends in the next village, some four kilometres away. My 'glutes' found it tough going as she strode along, chatting happily. I was nearly on my knees by the time we reached their house, only to find that the hoped-for lift home wasn't forthcoming. Her friends were out.

I confess to being quite pleased when Brett and Carol left at the end of the week as Carol kept getting attacks of helpless giggles which I found rather irritating. We all laugh at the memory years later, although my laughter is still rather rueful.

New wiring leading into
new fuse box

We worked really hard that week. When the new fuse box was finally installed with labelling in both French and English, giving us safe lighting and plenty of sockets, we celebrated by enjoying a hearty supper washed down by the local plonk – after dark!

During this week, David learned enough about French electrics to be brave enough to add outside lights and more sockets over subsequent years.

I, who, after my 'incident' with the ceiling had been demoted to safer tasks, spent the next couple of days staining the new windows and shutters, stripping wallpaper off doors (French chic?) and basically painting anything that didn't move - including Carol's nose. By the end of the holiday my hair was magnolia streaked with white and David had bloody fingers from drilling holes in walls and grouting the tiles. However we had safe electrics, two habitable bedrooms, an almost finished bathroom, and the dank smelly toilet was at last a nice place to be.

We had bought mosquito nets for our beds as my brother's house had been inundated with flies and bugs. However we never needed to use them as we found small mesh netting in 3MMM and David made a simple frame for each window (of course they were all different sizes) which could stay in place day and night, but could be taken down when the shutters were locked while we were away. We made hanging nets for the doors, fastened by Velcro, which kept any mosquitos and flies outside.

Two habitable bedrooms

Fortunately there weren't too many, even when sitting on the terrace in the evening, because the only farm in the village was arable. A nearby hamlet had a goat farm and their neighbour's swimming pool was virtually unusable due to the insects.

Previously when we'd stayed in France we had discovered that autumnal evenings could be chilly so we needed to think about heating before our next trip. We had already decided against central heating, so we bought half a dozen oil filled electric radiators instead. They have the advantage of being mobile (although you can remove the feet and fix them to walls) and have individual thermostatic controls. We found them effective and economical to run. Half an hour after turning on the radiator the bathroom was rendered cosy, even though it was large and uninsulated. Likewise the bedroom stayed warm all night with the thermostat turned to Very Low, even when there was snow outside. We did install a wood-burner in the main living room (*le sejour*) years later, but initially the radiators sufficed for our early spring and autumnal visits.

I have already touched on the fact that English houses are built differently to those in France, but the builders themselves are very similar. It's a fact that in both countries all building work will take longer and cost more than anticipated. The contractors' excuses in both countries are that the weather is 'wrong', they found more problems than anticipated, the deliveries are slow or 'wrong' and anyway the client – especially if he is English – has changed his mind. The client however, will say the builder didn't turn up, ordered items late, or did the work incorrectly so it had to be done again. Either way, it's the same result; late and over budget.

The French don't work in the rain. In England we are used to seeing builders slogging on in every weather; if they didn't projects would never be finished. In France if it rains the builders will work on an inside job; in the heat they will come back to finish outside. They also work a four-and-a-half-day week. They take two hours for lunch but don't stop for tea breaks. As strangers in a foreign country we have to accept these differences and learn to go with the flow or try to outwit them. Getting cross, shouting and throwing your arms around, does no good. It gives the Brits a bad name and causes the builder to disappear for months, leaving the job unfinished. Don't forget, he has your signature, you can't get anyone else to finish the job unless you are prepared to pay both him and the new contractor.

One advantage of the French system is that, when you employ a properly SIRET registered French builder, his costs can be added to the purchase price. So keep all your invoices to defray against Capital Gains Tax for when you or your beneficiaries sell the property. It is important to keep all paperwork as you may need to prove that such things as electrics and plumbing have been done in accordance with current standards.

Also important to know, the rate of TVA – the French equivalent of VAT – varies according to the type of work being undertaken. Renovation, replacement, repair and new work all carry differing percentages which I won't detail here as they are subject to governmental change. Your builder will apply the correct rates. So if you are renovating an existing house, TVA is charged at one rate; but if you are changing the use of the building it is different. Likewise if you are adding a new room or window, that will be rated as new work.

You may think of hiring a British builder to avoid the language problem, but be cautious. If he's working *sur le noir* (illegally or on the black) he won't have access to trade discounts and you won't be able to claim tax rebates for any work he does. Therefore unless he is properly registered with a SIRET number, best to avoid him except for very small jobs. We know of several people who hired unregistered British builders, and the main problem they encountered was that if the work wasn't satisfactory, they weren't covered by a contract and could not insist that the faults were made good.

TIPS AND INFORMATION

• *The French electrical system works on a spur system whereas the UK uses a ring circuit. Don't buy electrical fittings in England; they won't fit.*

• *Don't try and use ''sur le noir' (on the black) workmen.   Find contractors with a SIRET number. Good ones will have a lead-in time (possibly up to a year). Beware if they can start immediately.*

• *It is an offence to employ a member of your contractor's workforce on the sly. He could lose his job and you can be fined.*

• *In order to stick to your budget you need to make your requirements clear and not change your mind, so the builder then has to stick to his side of the contract.*

• *Be proactive; make decisions about finishes etc., in advance to reduce time waiting for items to be ordered.*

• *We needed to buy a gas hob so we could cook, although it would just be resting on trestles. Buy the matching oven at the same time, as designs change. Fortunately we did this, immediately checking it over although we stored it, re- packed, for another 18 months.*

• *Be honest with your contractor; if you're about to run out of money tell him so he can either stop work or offer a cheaper alternative. We made it clear at the outset that our budget was limited and our contractors were careful to keep within their devis (quotations). If we felt a quote was too expensive we asked if there was a cheaper alternative.   There usually was.*

• *Remember how delighted you were at the low property taxes when you bought the uninhabitable wreck?   Once you have renovated, your Tax D'Habitation and Tax Fonciere will double or more. The increase will be calculated on the number of bedrooms and toilets.*

• *Regarding taxes, unlike England where the TV licence is a separate item, the French include an 'aerial' tax in the annual Tax D'Habitation. If you don't have a TV and therefore an aerial, especially while you are renovating your property, you can deduct this amount from the invoice so you don't have to apply for a refund.   You will be required to sign a legal document confirming this fact, so please don't be tempted to lie; there are hefty penalties if you're caught.*

• *All 'devis' are EX TVA (the French equivalent of VAT).*

• *Obtain quotations from more than one contractor. Once you have chosen a builder, you can ask for prices for alternative details, eg, floors tiled either square or on the diagonal.   Ceilings with or without beams.   Different types of wood finishes, etc.   This way you can keep control of your budget.*

The view from our road
Chapter 10

We were busy all summer in the UK, spending every spare moment visiting charity shops for bargains, making lists of things to take with us, and of course deciding what jobs to tackle next. As usual, for our visit in September, our car groaned under the weight of our purchases which included tins of paint and tile adhesive that were cheaper in England. We even bought a Villager wood-burning stove in England – much against Mnsr le Plombier's wishes – we hadn't known chimney flues are different sizes in the two countries.

On our return to France we were pleased to note that the bathroom toilet had been installed, as had the shower fittings. Hot water at the push of a button. Such luxury. Indeed the new shower became a favourite place of retreat; we had chosen a large shower tray which gave us plenty of elbow room, and we loved standing under the flow of hot water for ages, in mindless inaction. Unless you have oil fired or Calor gas central heating your hot water tank will be heated by electricity with a non-adjustable thermostat which runs for 24 hours. So we bought a timer to plug into a wall socket; we could now heat the water when we wanted rather than all the time.

Because neither the bathroom nor the separate toilet had windows, we installed extractor fans as well as lights. It's wise to give the fans separate switches to the lights, as you won't want to have a noisy fan running if you need the loo in the middle of the night.

David carried on tiling the bathroom floor and walls while I continued painting in the bathroom, the hall, and the only kitchen wall already covered in plaster-board.

The shower in the tiled bathroom

At the same time our thoughts turned to actually fitting a kitchen instead of resting our gas hob on a pair of trestles and doing the washing up at the garden tap. I started measuring walls, doors and the window, and drew numerous designs on the backs of envelopes. However the final design had to wait until we'd decided which kitchen to buy.

Now that he had made and fitted the windows and shutters, our Main Man, he of the artistic nature, suggested a proper 'vestibule' leading from the kitchen to the bathroom. He also suggested adding another room leading off it, as he felt the garage area was far too large, being some 45 feet long by 25 feet wide and therefore wasted space. He described a vestibule area running from the kitchen to the bathroom at one end, the garage at the other end and a door to the new room opposite. This sounds complicated but made sense of an otherwise disconnected bathroom which was currently accessed via the garage.

A working bathroom

He told us the new room should measure 16' x 16' as plaster-board sheets come in 4 foot widths. Not having to cut them would save money and anyway, here he shrugged, Gaelic style, this was a good size for a room. We couldn't argue with his logic.

The new room couldn't have a window as it backed onto neighbour Andre's garden. We did explore the idea of a non-opening, opaque window but in the end thought a light tube from the roof through the loft into the ceiling would be a better idea.

The original vestibule -

left to the bathroom.   right to the garage

Some light tubes also open, giving ventilation to a room. Alternatively we could just install an extractor fan. We needed to investigate the costs before making a decision. Meantime our Main Man had his team begin work on the vestibule and new room, and I was able to prepare them for painting before we had to go home.

We called the new windowless room the *Cave* (cellar) so it would not be classed as a third bedroom and thus incur extra habitation taxes.

The finished vestibule

From the kitchen to   Looking left to the
the new room   bathroom

The new back room or Cave

However David had acquired a brass bedstead so we installed this, and some bookcases. It became my ironing and storage room despite being furnished as a bedroom.

Some furniture came via David's shop, some were people's cast-offs. The brass bedstead had been chucked into the store's skip one night; David saw that it only needed a new base so he brought it home and made wooden slats for it. The bedside tables came from a brother-in-law who was moving house, and the book cases were given to us by an English couple who were returning to the UK.

There was a wide opening in the kitchen block-work wall leading down into a large stone space which would become our living room or *sejour*. We decided this needed double doors and had thought of tiling the steps between the two, a drop of approximately one metre; but again, we liked our Main Man's suggestion of wooden steps, which sounded both attractive and cheaper.

Around this time Anna took us, with a mixed group of English and French, on a visit to a nearby town renowned for its ancient buildings and original streets. Tousson has featured in several films, including 'Chocolat' starring Juliette Binoche and Johnny Depp!

While we were admiring the museum artefacts I took photos of an arched window which I later showed to our Main Man. He liked the idea of double doors but warned that creating an arched frame would be expensive.

The internal double
doors and steps

So we compromised and everyone was delighted with the result. The soft wood beading creates a strong visual effect which still allows a lot of light, and the arched glass inside the standard door frame has that 'Wow' factor. I stained the steps, a hard wood without knots, with *Chene Clair* (clear oak).

Although we were given separate *devis* for the vestibule, new room, double doors and steps, we were invoiced for items completed rather than the whole job as we went home before the work was finished. On adding up everything later we think our Main Man went slightly over his estimates but the quality was of such a high standard that we didn't feel short changed. By this time he trusted us as much as we trusted his judgement, and he gave our works priority even when we weren't in residence.

TIPS AND INFORMATION

- *French taps and showers are designed to work from the French high pressure system, whereas England has low pressure mains water. Plumbing pipes are also different sizes in the two countries.*

- *It is worth sourcing items such as towel rails in UK - unless you find some in the sales in 3MMM.*

Poppies in the garden

Chapter 11

September was the best time for thinking about the garden, as the lawn was just recovering from the hot dry summer.   While out on one of the monthly *Randonees* (guided country walk) organised by Anna, which always ended with a sociable lunch in a local restaurant, we had met an English couple who mowed lawns.   They had happily agreed to mow our small patch of grass while we were away and now we turned to them for advice as to what we should plant for a hedge.   Currently we were separated from the road merely by chicken wire, and we yearned for privacy, especially when I breakfasted on our small terrace in my night-wear.

Chicken wire fence, no privacy

They recommended a plant nursery some miles away with the name of the required bush written down in French. The nursery was hidden away down some very narrow twisty lanes and we took several wrong turns before at last arriving, by now rather late in the afternoon. To our dismay it seemed deserted; then I spied a ship's style bell which, when pulled, jangled loudly. We stood waiting for several more minutes and at last a little man in very large wellington boots, staggered round the corner to greet us.

We explained who had sent us, and how many shrubs we needed. We quickly became aware that the only English Mnsr knew was 'no obligation' and as he proudly showed us around his well-stocked nursery, he kept up a running commentary on the plants, followed by this phrase. As he only spoke French we struggled to understand, and eventually realised he was encouraging us to buy more than we had come for, by the repetition of his phrase 'no obligation'. However we stuck to our guns (we had to, we'd only brought enough cash for the shrubs we wanted) and at last managed to load a dozen healthy plants into the car. He had one last attempt to sell us compost, but as we'd brought a dozen bags of well-rotted horse manure (I have horses) from UK, we escaped without purchasing any. Well, he had insisted there was 'no obligation'.

The next few evenings were spent planting these bushes, which activity seemed to excite our neighbours who all came along to watch and offer helpful comments. They were the right shrubs to plant as they tolerated neglect well and quickly bushed out to create a suitable barrier from the road.

Our hedge fully grown after a couple of years

While we were busy in the garden, the steps from the kitchen to the lower part of the barn were being installed, so at the same time our thoughts now turned to the untouched *sejour*. This was a long, rather dank, space – some forty feet – which made the far end from the French doors very dark.

There was already a gaping hole in the far end wall, which we were allowed to infill as a window; but it had to be restricted to a non-opening, opaque glass because it overlooked Andre's garden. For the same reason permission would not be granted to make a new window in the long external wall.

In order to gain more light in this room, we decided to create a completely new window, overlooking our own garden, next to the French doors. This needed a mason to knock a hole in the stone wall, and of course our Main Man would make the new window and shutters.

So off we trotted to Mnsr le Maire to obtain permission for the new window. He made the application on our behalf, using a digital camera to show 'before' and 'after' pictures. This was very helpful as he filled out all the forms and sent off the paperwork on our behalf. To be fair, I expect he wanted to make sure it was done properly. We were rather surprised but very pleased that we didn't have to pay anything for the application.

The picture Mnsr le Maire submitted for
our new window

The design had to be in the *style Charentaise* as this external alteration was within 300 metres of the protected 12th century church, so special permission was sought from the French Heritage office in Paris. It pays to keep the mayor on your side as he has the authority to put forward permissions, or even to refuse them without recourse to higher officials. Fortunately ours was a forward looking chap who liked the English delicacies we brought.

During that winter, permission was granted. The mason and the carpenter submitted their quotations by e-mail. We signed and returned them, hoping works would commence in our absence.

Needless to say, they didn't.

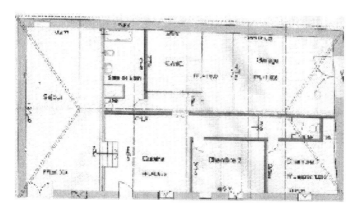

Showing the completed layout.
The double-dash lines show the roof structure,
the solid black lines are block-work walls.
The brown walls are external stone and
insulated internal block-work walls.

Now permission for the new window was in hand, with work progressing well on internal steps and double doors, our thoughts could turn to choosing kitchen units. I was heartily tired of washing up in the garden, with the old sink balanced on trestles, and guests always picked at their food gingerly, as though they expected to contract some terrible disease.

The original kitchen

In England I had worked for a Civil Engineer who specialised in domestic repairs required after subsidence, slippage and heave damage, which gave me an insight into building practices. I was currently working in an architects' studio, where I saw on a daily basis the importance of site management as well as how to plan and order work. I knew about unusual solutions to problems such as light tubes into a dark room, the importance of ventilation, and how to plan a kitchen and bathroom layout. So when I wanted to plan our new kitchen, I made sure I had all the necessary measurements to hand; ceiling height, length of walls, position of window, door, pipes and electric meter, as well as the width of our fridge freezer.

I then made a sketch using these measurements; it wasn't to scale or even pretty, but showed accurate distances and included the appliances we needed.

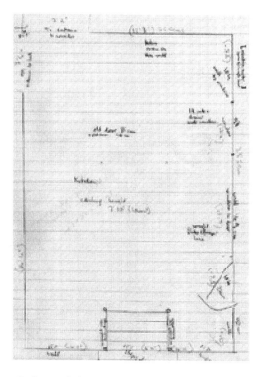

It doesn't have to be pretty, just have accurate measurements

Back at home, I studied every kitchen catalogue I could lay my hands on, so when our first grandchild was born that autumn, a Christmas visit to her in the Midlands enabled me to call in to the Nottingham/Derby branch of Ikea. Using my rough sketch and detailed measurements they designed an L-shaped kitchen full of the appropriate cupboards, drawers, corner carrousel and pull-out larder. Armed with this plan we visited other UK kitchen suppliers to compare prices before deciding finally on the Ikea units, which had been my favourite all along.

So in the third year since buying the barn, our Easter visit to France saw us heading for the Bordeaux Ikea (there is one in Tours too) where we placed our order for the kitchen units. The French assistant took our English print-out and promised they would phone my mobile as soon as they had a definite delivery date, which would be approximately six weeks hence. Ordering the items was made much easier by having the plan already designed as the French assistant didn't speak any English. They had to change the catalogue numbers however, as these were different in the French branch.

Our weekends in England had become a trawl around the DIY stores, reclamation yards, charity shops and the local tip for anything that might come in handy, One day we were prowling the aisles of a local DIY shop when my mobile rang.

"Bonjour, ici Ikea en Bordeaux,' a French voice introduced himself. I quickly found a quiet corner for the conversation.

'Ah, bonjour….' Mouthing to David, 'It's Ikea,' I quickly switched language to French, hoping that I would manage to hold up my end of the conversation. Relaying my credit card details down the phone whilst sitting in the kitchen department of a rival store in England felt surreal and exciting rather than embarrassing. Bubbling with excitement and replaying the conversation over and over, we rushed out of the shop, eager to plan our next visit to France.

With the delivery date now set in stone, we booked a three week holiday in June to give ourselves time to prepare the kitchen walls before the units arrived, and then to install them before we had to leave again. Thankfully the previous owner had already tiled the kitchen floor so that was one job we didn't have to worry about. We also rang our Main Man to insist he complete plaster-boarding the kitchen to allow sufficient time to paint the walls before fitting the units.

Needless to say, he didn't ! Are you noticing a theme here?

TIPS AND INFORMATION

• *When choosing shrubs and plants for your garden, ensure they will cope with the local climate, and with being neglected while the property is shut.*

- *If you plant a hedge, check how quickly it will grow as you probably won't want to be continually cutting it back.*

- *If you're not sure what to plant, look around the local area and see which plants are doing well in that micro-climate.*

The original kitchen

Chapter 12

Boy, that was a hectic three weeks. The new back room and vestibule were being finished while David and I ripped out the remaining grotty kitchen fittings.

Ripping out the last of the old kitchen fittings

Joel, our Main Man's top plasterer, had a great sense of humour; to my horror he said they would arrive at 7 o'clock the next morning. I thought he was joking.

Because many rural houses keep a guard dog either chained or roaming in their 'yards', trying to ring a door bell would mean running the gauntlet of these unwelcoming animals. Therefore the French have a bell, or bell pull, at the gate, with a wire running into the house. The owner can then control the dog before letting in the visitor. At that time we hadn't installed any bell, anywhere, so I was startled (to say the least) when Joel began whistling loudly as he passed our bedroom window, knocking on the partially open shutters, giving me time to struggle into shorts and T shirt before I let him in – just as the church bells began their 7 o'clock clarion.

The mobile hob   Washing up in the garden

I needed to quickly paint the new plaster-board walls (one PVA coat and two magnolia) and the same in a white finish on the ceiling, which meant dancing around

Joel as he ran up and down a ladder installing plaster-board on the kitchen ceiling, so David could then fit the new spotlights.

Joel skimming the new
plaster-board walls

Fitting spotlights into
the new ceiling

We continually moved the fridge and hob from one place to another as we all manoeuvred around the room. By now the old kitchen sink was permanently on trestles in the garden, with a hose attachment from the outside tap.

All too soon, the designated delivery day for the kitchen units arrived, and at 10 o'clock there was a knock on the garage door. It took both us and the two beefy delivery men about half an hour to unload and check everything. After the lorry had left, we stood with Joel and his assistant, looking at the boxes piled high in the garage and gulped. Laughing, they wished us *bon chance* and slapped David on his back as they disappeared on their lunch break.

By this time in our renovation we had realised that no floor was level, no corner was 90 degrees and no wall was quite straight, so, never one to rush into things, David took a considerable time working out where to start.   To pass the time while waiting for his decision, I poured us yet another cold drink.

We decided the floor corner unit was key. Opening the appropriate box we took deep breathes and prepared to start. First we found and laid out a rug as suggested in the instructions, then we collected all the necessary tools. David had experience of building furniture from flat packs so was able to follow the diagrams easily. Unfortunately that first box we opened didn't have the pack of fixings in it.   Good old Anna to the rescue again! She helped me ring Ikea and place an order for the necessary items, but to my horror they would not arrive for another two weeks. We had no choice but to raid the other units so we could progress.

The first
cupboard in
place

As we gained confidence we built the cupboards more quickly, with fewer arguments and broken fingernails. Once all the floor cupboards were finished we pushed them against the walls. Then we began on the wall units. But – sensibly as it happened – we didn't attach any to the walls as, on slotting them into the designated positions, we realised we'd forgotten to position a double-door floor cupboard next to the oven/hob unit to house the gas bottle; so the oven unit needed to be moved one cupboard to the left, which meant also adjusting the wall cupboards.

Getting there

Working on into the night, we managed to assemble all the cupboards; then, using chairs, books and blocks of wood on which to balance the wall units, we shifted them around until they were in the proper sequence. At this point we called a halt, relaxing on the terrace with a much needed long cool drink, watching the bats swooping overhead and the stars and planes high in the night sky. Next morning, refreshed, we continued to the really stressful bit; fastening them in place. It quickly became apparent that not only was the floor uneven, so were the walls. David had to make wedges to screw into the walls to level up the cupboards.

Fixing the wall units before the floor cupboards worked best as this allowed us more space to manoeuvre the step ladder. David carefully measured the distance from the yet-to-be-installed worktop to the bottom of the wall cupboards so the wall tiles (we had already chosen 4" square tiles) would fit between the work surface and the wall cupboards without needing to be cut.

Have you ever tried cutting kitchen work-tops? Neither had we. Our jig-saw was not strong enough to make a clean cut in a straight line, so after we had spoilt one end, we panicked and called our Main Man who sent his lad over with the biggest circular saw imaginable. We ate green dust (it was a green worktop) for several days after but he did a grand job.

Then the plumber arrived to fit the sink, only to find that the unit needed trimming to fit the new double sink and drainer. Ah, well, that was only a minor problem as problems go and easily resolved. But we did wonder whether we would manage to finish installing the cupboards before it was time to go home.

The cupboards in the right places

Years later, we still admired our handiwork and the ingenuity required to fit it. I am quite tall and wanted my worktops at a height which left a gap between the kicking board and floor, and David had the brilliant idea of using the under-wall cupboards valence to join the kicking board to the bottom of the units. It worked a treat and looked as though it was a design feature. (Well, it was, just our design feature rather than the manufacturer's).

The completed kitchen

The other end of the kitchen

TIPS AND INFORMATION

• *Measure everything several times, then measure again. Most kitchen departments will design your kitchen units on their computers. Don't skimp on 'fancy' things like pull out larders, carousels, etc. The amount you would save is negligible compared to the overall cost of the conversion.*

• *If your sink is to be below the window remember French windows open inwards so measure the height of the tap very carefully. You don't want to restrict the window's movement.*

• *When your old stone house / barn was built, they didn't use spirit levels. If you use a spirit level to fit your cupboards, they won't look right.*

• *Worktops are very difficult to cut. Also very messy. Try and do it out of doors. You need to rest the worktop on a strong, stable, level surface.*

• *Choosing the wall tiles before you fit the kitchen wall cupboards will reduce the amount of tile cutting needed. Then allow for the depth of the worktop and the grouting when you measure the distance to the wall cupboards.*

- *If you have already tiled the bathroom, various floors, etc., change the blade on the tile cutter. It's most likely blunt.*

- *Tiling the interior window sills makes them easier to clean and stops the plaster-board from getting wet.*

- *If you have a gas hob remember to arrange for a large floor cupboard next to it for the Calor gas bottle. These bottles are available from the local supermarket, eg, LeClerc or similar. You have to pay a deposit for the first bottle which allows you to buy just the gas when you go for a refill.*

- *An electric oven needs a special electric socket, with a heavy duty cable. For ease of access we fitted ours in the cupboard which housed the gas bottle, as they should both be turned off when the house is empty.*

- *At this point – if not earlier – you will realise you have an odd cable coming into the house from the electric pump for the septic tank. Ours came up under the sink so we led it along under the units to a socket in the gas bottle cupboard, again allowing easy access for when it needed to be switched off while the house was closed up.*

The village *lavoir* (wash house)
Chapter 13

We finished fitting the kitchen at 2am, knowing we had a six-hour drive before catching the evening ferry home. We fell into bed, exhausted but triumphant. Four hours sleep and a hot shower apiece later, we headed off, with dirty sheets and damp towels bundled into the car for laundering at home. We were utterly shattered after our 'holiday' and even slept upright on the ferry, but after three years at last we had a shiny clean kitchen. Our friends and neighbours would no longer have to worry about food poisoning when we entertained!

The cupboards may not have their knobs and handles yet and the walls weren't tiled, but we knew we'd have time to complete that before David's parents came to stay the following spring. It had taken me ages to find tiles that complemented the cupboards and worktop, that we both liked and at the right price (that's the difficult bit) and even then they cost more than our original budget; but at least we only needed four boxes rather than the fifteen the bathroom walls had required.

David's early retirement allowed him to visit France on his own, so he went the following February in order to get ahead with some chores he could undertake alone. He was a bit nervous about driving 400 miles – approximately six and a half hours – on his own, while I was more concerned about his idea on self-catering; I packed him several home cooked frozen meals and plenty of tea bags and happily waved him off. After all, I not only had an office to manage but three horses and a daughter at home and another son at a nearby university (who kept coming home). I was looking forward to catching up on my reading, and having the whole bed to myself.

Tiles and miniature buckets

I was at work when I received a frantic phone call. How did I want the three colours of kitchen wall tiles set out? He couldn't get the numbers to work, and couldn't find the design I'd sorted out during our last visit. Fortunately I had photographed the pattern and loaded it onto my laptop, so I was able to e-mail the picture to Anna. When I flew out to join him a couple of weeks later, I was suitably impressed with the completed kitchen; he'd even hung the French chicken with hooks and buckets I'd given him for Christmas.

During one such solo visit, David was undertaking a fairly quiet job when he realised he could hear a strange buzzing sound, rather like an electrical fizz. He ignored it at first but eventually felt he had to search it out. He climbed the ladder into the loft space and was horrified to find a huge nest of swarming hornets. He beat a rapid retreat and dashed over to Anna to ask her how best to tackle this invasion.

Loft space

'You'll have to call out the *Pompiers* (fire brigade),' she said. 'Hornets can deliver lethal stings. If you receive even one sting, you must go straight to the hospital, so we'll ring for help now and stay well clear until the nest has been dealt with.'

When the firemen arrived, they were dressed from head to toe in protective clothing; not even a finger was left uncovered. They told David to shut all windows and doors and wait in the kitchen while they sprayed the nest. It took quite a while for the poisonous spray to disperse so David had supper with Anna. She truly was our Guardian Angel. He then spent several days sweeping and vacuuming all the dead bodies, some of which had managed to find their way into the house before dying.

The *Pompiers* charged 60€.

David was also alone one cold February when it snowed hard. One day there was a timid knock on the door.   He opened it to find Andre, our French neighbour, who wanted to ask him to lunch.   So at 12 noon David presented himself at Andre's door, where he was greeted with a large glass of Pineau – the local aperitif of wine fortified by cognac – before sitting down to the first course. David didn't speak much French, and Andre's English was rusty, but they got on really well with the use of *Franglais* and lots of gestures. They had a rich red Burgundy to accompany the meat and cheese courses, followed by a sweet white with the desert. By this time, David was rather full and quite tipsy but Andre was still going strong.

Andre had been evacuated to New York during the second world war after his Jewish parents had 'disappeared' from Paris at the hands of the Germans. He had led a fascinating if difficult life since then and was now on his own.   He relished a new male neighbour to chat to and with whom to practise his English. He made coffee and pressed a whisky or two on David as they sat in front of the log fire.   It was several hours later that David managed to extricate himself, and even then he found Andre accompanying him home. By this time they were both somewhat worse for wear and for some unknown reason, they decided to pay Anna a social visit. She rang me, giggling, to tell me that she hadn't managed to eject the two men from her house until about nine that evening and even then she'd cautiously watched them weave their wobbly way to their respective homes.

It snowed heavily that night so David was surprised when Anna knocked on the door the next day; she'd received a phone call from Andre asking if they could have lunch again soon. He'd rung her because he didn't want to risk the slippery slope up to the barn. David was still suffering the after effects from the day before's rather liquid lunch. He panicked. His digestive system wouldn't cope with another marathon food and drink fest. There and then he made the decision that he was going home. The following morning he was on the road, despite the snow being two feet deep along the country lanes and not a snow plough in sight!

Minus 10 degrees C

Since then, we've become close friends with Andre, but we've learned to exercise restraint when we dine with him!

When David's parents came to stay for a few days that summer, we gave ourselves a rest from work. Instead we relaxed and enjoyed showing them around the area, taking them to the large fortnightly market in Rouillac, visiting the Roman amphitheatre nearby and enjoying lunch in our favourite *Rellais* restaurant in Aigre. However their preferred entertainment was to sit on the terrace under the parasol, with a glass of something cool and a selection of local cheeses.

Enjoying the sunshine on the small terrace

Pa-in-Law discovered the cognac we'd bought from a local farmer, Jean-Yves, who had his own still in his *cellier* (cellar). One night I woke to hear rustling in the kitchen. I thought perhaps we had a mouse so crept quietly down the hall. There was Pa with a glass in one hand and my secret stash of dark chocolate KitKats in the other, having an illicit midnight feast. We had to laugh.

Over the last few years we'd given each other presents of such things as fancy wrought iron coat hooks, a weathervane, pictures found in charity shops, as well as ornaments to fit in niches and crannies, and these were duly hung/displayed as each room was finished.

Phase One, which was originally meant to take just one year, was nearing completion after three years; at the beginning of Year Four we only had one room left to do.

Or that was what we thought.

The stone space, open to the roof

This was still a bare space, open to the roof, of some fifty square metres. David said no way could he tile the floor, it would take him years and his knees would never recover. So our Main Man found us a *carreleur* (tiler) who supplied us with his *devis* but insisted he couldn't do anything until the new window was installed. Also he wanted the ceiling fitted, the walls plaster-boarded and the wooden steps finished so his new tiles wouldn't be damaged by these works. So we urged the Main Man to crack the whip at the Mason and create the window for which they had quoted a whole year earlier.

We couldn't create a new window on the long external wall as that overlooked Andre's property, but thankfully there was already a gaping hole in the far end wall, which we were allowed to infill as a window. Unfortunately it had to be restricted to a non-opening, opaque glass because it overlooked Andre's garden, but our Main Man happily turned this ugly hole into a smart window which gave some light to that end of the room.

The finished window, non-opening,
opaque, overlooking Andre's garden.

Internal   External

TIPS AND INFORMATION

- Be careful not to spend so much on renovating that you outstrip the local market. The French property market doesn't increase in value in the same way as in the UK, and it's very easy to make your renovation too elaborate for the locale. We know of a couple who hired an architect, only used the 'best' (most expensive) materials to convert a barn and old stone house, only to lose heavily (approximately £100,000) when they had to sell.

- We were lucky in having a nearby airport in England which offered cheap flights to both Limoges and La Rochelle; this made it affordable and easy for me to join David when he'd driven there alone.

- If you intend to run a B&B or let out gites, be aware of what local facilities you can offer. It's no good creating a Boutique gite unless you have a swimming pool or easy access to a beach.

- It's tempting to transform an unused roof space into several en suite bedrooms, but it's unlikely that your family will all come to stay at the same time, and your taxes will increase along with the number of bedrooms and bathrooms.

- *And remember that when you advertise your gite, you are in direct competition with the ferry companies who offer package deals which includes discounted travel with their accommodation.*

- *Running a business, even a one-bed gite for a couple of months a year, requires a lot of jumping through bureaucratic hoops. So you need to work out the finances very carefully before you begin.*

A damp and dark stone room
Chapter 14

Because our contractors were now accustomed to our schedule of May and September visits, they agreed to start work creating the new window in our absence. Anna was able to send more photos; this time showing the sequence of solid wall, hole in the wall with Acro props, then larger hole with more Acro props, followed by the lintel making its way down the path.

Hole in the wall with Acro props

That poor wheelbarrow

I felt so sorry for the poor wheelbarrow which seemed to sag under the weight of the huge stone lintel that took four men to manhandle into place.

As ever, Anna proved a valuable friend 'on the ground'. We rang her most days and she was generous with her time, keeping us informed. With her keeping an eye on the work we knew the barn was in safe hands. At last the props were removed, to reveal a proper window complete with dressed stone surround. We were glued to the computer for a whole week.

The new window, awaiting shutters

By this time we had considerable faith in our Main Man's opinion and experience. He ensured we didn't make the common mistake of leaving the sejour open to the roof. We would never be able to heat it, he said, and anyway the roof rafters weren't even pretty or vintage.

Stone space open to the roof

Better by far to put in a sensible ceiling, he'd install beams if we insisted, but they would make a dark room even darker. He's been proved right; we compromised on the height of the ceiling (higher than he wanted, lower than I wanted), painted it white without beams but with lots of spotlights, fans, and a brass chandelier to make it interesting. We loved its modern chic look and visitors all said 'wow'.

Fully painted with spot lights in the
floating ceiling channel

At last the window, ceiling and plasterboard walls were done. All that was left to do was to find an electrician to lead wires behind the new plaster-board for sockets, switches and aerial points, after which it would be ready for me to paint. Our Main Man said his usual electrician had retired but eventually he found a newly qualified man who agreed to supply us with a *devis*.

The ceiling is about 14 feet high. Some people can manage long-handled rollers, but I find they tend to veer out of control so I ended up on the step ladder with a short-handled roller and backache, neck ache, arm ache and foot ache.

135

The first coat (PVA) was painful, the second (white paint) was agony and I was in tears half way through the third. David had to keep me plied with cold drinks -– soft in case I fell off the ladder – and rousing music on the CD player. At last the floor could be tiled.

Furnished, floor tiled on the diagonal.
Viewed from the kitchen end

Viewed from the 'dark' end

We Brits love stone walls, inside as well as out. If they are attractive by all means keep them. However, this was a barn, originally built to house animals. The stonework was rough and in places had been tanked with ugly cement to combat damp. The 'mortar' used on old barns was a mixture of manure and grasses; not particularly healthy as it leaks spores and dust. The internal walls recently added were breeze block, some covered with dark and dismal wallpaper, others had dark paint. We covered all the breeze block and most of the stone walls with plaster-board to achieve a clean and healthy finish.

It looked fabulous. We were particularly proud of our 'floating ceiling' effect that hid a number of spotlights which washed the one remaining stone wall with soft down-lighting. None of the other walls were attractive enough to leave exposed so we took the opportunity to hide them behind plaster-board, adding insulation at the same time.

Our son was working part time in a hotel that threw away two ceiling fans during a refurbishment. So he 'rescued' them in our direction. They went in really easily and as well as sending warm air through the house when the wood burner was lit, had the added advantage of sending cool air through the whole ground floor when reversed in the summer.

Ceiling fans and a chandelier, ceiling spots and wall lights gave several possible lighting combinations which changed the mood of the room. We were thrilled with the effect, especially once I installed my large desk, positioned right beneath the new window. We also hung a large arched mirror at the 'dark' end to reflect light, which was very effective.

It was the plumber's job to install the wood-burning stove and chimney. Again, because of our proximity to the 12th Century church, we had to gain permission for a tall chimney to finish above the roof ridge height. Our favourite Mayor made this easy, but insisted that the chimney could not be shiny silver metal. He wanted it to be clad in stone or brick, but the plumber thought that would be too heavy and necessitate reinforcing the roof beams. Instead he found a cream metal chimney stack which was deemed acceptable.

Initially we'd planned to find a grandiose stone fireplace and mantle in one of the many reclamation yards. However this idea came to nought.

The free standing
burner

The cream chimney

Once the wood burner was installed we decided we loved the spare look of the stove with its black flue, free standing away from the wall, without a fireplace surround. Instead we stood its legs on slices of logs to protect the floor tiles, and piled a few logs underneath. The room is very modern with its spotlights and smooth cream walls, so we now felt an antique stone fireplace would look out of place. This was particularly fortunate decision as we were running out of money!

Because our renovation had taken so long, we'd had time to get the 'feel' of the house and how it worked for us. This allowed us to change our minds from some original ideas and incidentally often choose the cheaper option. If Phase One had really taken only one year, we would have made several expensive mistakes.

Before we could use the wood burner, we needed logs. Again our Guardian Angel Anna came to the rescue and sent local farmer Jean-Yves to us with a trailer full of logs. He arrived mid-morning and dumped them in the middle of the road before sitting down in our bright shiny kitchen where he proceeded to substantially lower the level of a bottle of Pineau, while David and I rushed to remove the logs from the road and stack them neatly in the garage before the neighbours complained. We did have to pay for the logs but delivery just cost half a bottle of *Pineau*.

Neatly stacked logs in the garage

We had met Jean-Yves the previous year, when Anna had driven us to his farm in the next hamlet. He'd invited us into his *cellier*, a sort of dug-out beneath his house, with stone walls, earthen floor, cobweb festooned wooden ceiling, and a couple of wonky shelves, on which balanced several dusty jars and other debris. There were also two large vats of cognac, home brewed of course. We perched on an uncomfortable selection of stools and J-Y rubbed his grubby thumb around the inside of some jam jars before pouring us each a liberal dose of smooth cognac.

This was at 10 o'clock in the morning and Jean-Yves seemed to be in no hurry for us to drink up and leave. Our French improved with each sip; as our inhibitions relaxed so our conversational skills grew. I think J-Y even understood some of what we said! At last it was time to leave as J-Y's wife informed us that his lunch was ready. We staggered out with the couple of bottles he'd very kindly allowed us to buy, and giggled like school children as Anna's car took us home. Indeed it was a good thing the car knew where it was going, as Anna was certainly not capable of concentrating.

FRENCH REMEDY FOR A COLD
Take a candle and a bottle of cognac to bed.
Light the candle. Drink the cognac.
When you see 2 flames, blow them both out.
Sleep until morning.

TIPS AND INFORMATION

• *Don't be afraid to adjust your ideas; the great thing about taking your time is you get a feel for how the house will work for you.*

• *When the electrician installs the wiring, ask for some spare cables to be left attached to the fuse box, so you can add more sockets and lights as you realise you've under estimated. Also, make sure he threads the cables under the upstairs floor boards / ceiling* joists for ease of movement in the loft or future first floor rooms.

- Stone houses tend to have small windows so white ceilings help to brighten the interior.

- English chimney flues are a different size to French, either bring out the whole flue or buy a French wood burner. Check the efficiency of the various burners as some use more wood than others. We were very pleased with our Villager stove, which we took out from England. French wood burners have improved a lot over recent years.

- By lucky chance we had enough room to store our stairs of logs in the attached garage, which is accessed through the vestibule. Our friends who had to brave icy conditions or rain in order to replenish theirs, were extremely jealous.

Work in progress, new terrace

Chapter 15

So there we were, four years on and pretty much finished with Phase One indoors; not that you ever finish with an old house. There were of course the final touches: fixing an outside light or two, re-staining the external woodwork on alternate years, adding a high decorative shelf in the toilet, laying insulation in the roof space, putting up hooks in the workshop / garage etc. The list seemed endless and we had thought we'd nearly finished.

At last David could tile all the window sills: I had found four Moroccan tiles in a sale basket, for just 50 cents each.   Brightly coloured patterns in blue and yellow, they were a challenge to match, but eventually I found plain blue and yellow tiles to make a really attractive sill in our bedroom.   David had extended the kitchen wall tiles onto the window sill, and the sills in the *sejour* were also tiled.   If the inward opening windows were open when it rained, the sills got wet.   The tiles also saved them from fly droppings when the house was shut up.

Tiled window sills

Our bedroom still had a 'hole in the wall' cavity, which David had plaster-boarded then added shelves and a rail to make a hanging cupboard. It was too narrow for a standard door and I'd been happy to leave it open for ventilation.   Back in England we found a white-wood louvered door which would fit.   This was another moment when carrying measurements with me at all times was so useful.   Unfortunately the door was six feet tall and wouldn't fit into our car.   David very carefully cut it in half, creating dowel holes so he'd be able to join it up again.

Once painted, David joined the two halves together. He used hinges taken from an armoire which had been left in the barn (too damaged to save) and a handle we'd salvaged from the worm ridden piano we'd chopped up several years earlier, thus retaining some of the barn's history. It looked great when finished and even better, only cost £15 and some lateral thinking.

At last we could turn our thoughts to things external. David had released a rusty garden table from a skip in England; he had taken this back to bare metal before painting it a lovely dark green. One of the French garden centres had a sale of furniture where we found several chairs really cheaply. A reduced price parasol completed the ensemble and we now had time to enjoy the terrace with a bottle of something cool and a bowl of olives. What more could one ask for?

Well, for a start, fewer weeds and some trees. A mower to help turn the meadow into *a* lawn – that was in a sale too. Perhaps some ornaments to hide the septic tank. Visits to local *Brocantes* and even *Emmaus* soon sorted that.

Stone wall around the electric pump hatch

David built a stone wall around the electric pump lid to make it look like an old well, and I planted succulents in the cracks. With more time to sit around entertaining, we discovered that our terrace was really too narrow for the table and four chairs.

I had been diligently moving the random piles of stone into a heap at the far end of the garden, so we (he) decided we would use these stones as the base for a wider terrace. I lugged wheelbarrow load after wheelbarrow load of stones back across the garden while David built the stone wall. I gave thanks that the garden was no bigger.

New terrace and rockery

With a little scavenging of abandoned stones along the roadsides, we had just about enough to create a retaining wall and infill an area of about 3 metres by 4 metres, by which time my arms felt about 6 feet long ! Then all we had to do was head off to the local Brico depot and buy several trailer loads of *calcaire* – a useful mixture of stone and chalk that hardens when wet.

Of course we couldn't get the trailer into the garden so again 'we' filled the wheelbarrow many times before depositing the *calcaire* onto the rubble base, raking it smooth. Five or so years later, we still had a pleasant terrace bounded by an attractive stone wall, and a path delineated by more stones. I was near to tears with exhaustion by the end of that day, but David was right to push us to finish, even though I would have walked off site for ever – if I'd had the energy.

The upside is two-fold; we are proud of having built the terrace and stone walls ourselves, and – almost more importantly – it cost us hardly anything. It became our favourite sun trap for breakfast as well as lunch, evening drinks and star gazing. On sunny summer days we even recorded temperatures reaching 40*C.

The new terrace

TIPS AND INFORMATION

- *It may take time for all those things you wanted to throw away, to come into their own. The stones had been littering the garden, making mowing the grass difficult. Never throw them away; old stones are very desirable; large ones are like gold dust.*

- *When choosing plants for your garden, think about when you will be in residence. We planted masses of spring bulbs but never saw them; instead the neighbours told us how pretty they had looked. If you don't want to spend all your time in the garden, go for long lasting bright flowers in tubs; scarlet geraniums last all summer and give an instant lift to the garden. Also succulents on a rockery make an attractive, low maintenance feature.*

- *We were only able to visit a few times each year so, to keep the neighbours happy, we organised for the lawn to be mowed in our absence; this is another, albeit minor, expense to consider.*

- *If you want a land phone line, you can ask the telephone company to turn it off while you aren't in residence, which saves on standing charges.*

- *Make sure you read the meters when you first arrive and as you leave; your bills (water and electricity) might be estimated or read as though you're in permanent residence, so you need to be able to check the amount even when you're in the UK.*

- *There's a saying: you only need two things in life: if it's supposed to move and doesn't, use WD40; if it's not supposed to move and it does, use gaffer tape.*

However some other bits of kit are essential when renovating: a portable work bench, an electric tile cutter, a re-chargeable drill with stone bits, Silicone spray and a trade Henry-style vacuum cleaner, preferably one which tolerates water as well as dust/ rubble.   Latex gloves, strong gardening gloves, overalls and face masks for handling woodworm / insulation / weed killers.

- *A First Aid kit is also useful and a good quality corkscrew is essential.*

Relaxing on the new terrace

Chapter 16

I may have given you the erroneous impression that it never rained while we were in residence. The weather in the Charente is similar to that in the south of England, but warmer and sometimes wetter. We suffered the occasional downpour; one morning I was woken by the sound of a waterfall outside our bedroom. When I swung my legs out of bed, I was horrified as my feet plunged into ice cold water, making me squeal loudly and wake David. He was most unimpressed to find the floor was flooded. The barn was downhill of the road so we were used to some water ingress beneath the garage door, but to have it coming into the bedroom was a different matter. We had always been aware of occasional damp patches on the roadside bedroom wall, but this was much more serious.

We quickly cleared the floor, picking up the soaked rugs and hanging them in the garage to dry. Thankfully the rain had stopped so I was able to mop up, allowing us to keep the damage to a minimum. We pondered how to attack the problem over breakfast, eventually agreeing on a plan of action.

David removed the sodden plaster-board internal wall. We could immediately see huge gaps between the wall stones, below the level of the pavement outside. He promptly filled these holes with small stones then sealed the wall with cement and the waterproof adhesive he'd used on the floor tiles in the bathroom. The new plaster-board wall then had to have the usual coat of PVA followed by two of paint.

This laminate flooring in the bedrooms had been laid when we bought the barn. We had never liked it but with so many jobs to do, it was low on the list of things to replace. Now however it was beyond saving. We made a quick trip to Monsieur Bricolage in Ruffec which had a sale. There we found enough tiles at half price to lay new floors in both bedrooms. David spent a couple of days tiling our bedroom but the second floor had to wait as he said his knees were giving out. This led to him deciding he didn't want to be a tiler when he grew up. Mind you, he had said the same about being an electrician when he was hanging outside lights, nor a plumber when he had to unblock drains. To be honest, he still hasn't decided what he wants to be when he grows up!

Starting to lay the tiles on the bedroom floor

Given the wet weather, it was fortunate that we had just commissioned the guttering, which had been one of the last professional jobs on our list for Phase One. The roof was large and the rain gushed off it, leading to damp patches around the windows and where the stone walls needed re-pointing. Our plumber had given us a quote for this work 3 years earlier, which he now decided he didn't want to do as he felt too old to climb ladders. I think he'd had problems fitting the chimney! So he introduced us to his son-in-law who had been his apprentice. Once more the Heritage area surrounding the 12th Century church meant we weren't allowed any plastic externally, so Young Plumber happily gave us a new, more expensive *devis* for fixing much larger galvanised gutters. We gulped a bit but signed it on the understanding that the work would be complete by our next visit. Amazingly, for once, it was.

The only time we had a problem with water after that was when the new guttering became filled with leaf debris, blocking the down-pipe. Thankfully that was an easy fix. At this time, we decided to make an effort to keep water out of the garage so we bought some drain guttering which we dug into the gravel pavement outside the garage door. It took several goes to get the height and position exactly right, but eventually did the trick.

Although all the major works had now been done, there were still plenty of small jobs to complete. I painted the plaster-board covering the back garage wall, then PVA'd the garage concrete floor (one part PVA to three parts water) to keep down the dust.

Tidy garage with dry sealed floor

We (well, me, complete with overalls, mask, and a very, very long ladder) treated the roof rafters for woodworm.

The roof space was huge, with six enormous rafters spanning it, and lots of supporting beams, purlins and trusses. The snow lining under the tiles, although torn in places, kept out the rain where the tiles had moved. I had been rather anxious about the vertical king pins as they didn't seem to fit flush with the centre of the horizontal beam. However our Main Man soon put me right. Because France experiences such extreme temperatures, the wooden rafters have to be able to expand and contract. So the vertical joint is left with about 4" of movement. If this gap is permanently reduced, it means the whole roof is moving and needs attention

Roof rafters

The gap allowing for movement

David made a new gate and tidied up the hedges and fences. He wired in external lights and hung a manual door bell. We even strung a washing line in the garage for wet days. The metal garage doors needed some TLC; they were dented in places and rather rusty. David carefully bashed out the dents and prepared them for painting. Once more the Heritage area restricted the selection of colours we were allowed; I chose the dark (British Racing) green, but David found a tin of metal paint at half price. The doors were painted grey.

Around this time, at a *brocante*, we found several boxes of plinth (or skirting) tiles at a bargain price. David decided they would neaten the join between the tiled floor and the plaster-board walls in various rooms, one of which was the small toilet. After all, this was such a small room it wouldn't take long; perhaps just a morning. Trying to wriggle around behind the loo, he managed to dislodge the china toilet roll holder which fell, smashing on the floor. I hoovered up the shards while David repaired the holes in the wall which I then repainted. So now we had to find a new loo-roll holder; fortunately *Emmaus* was open that afternoon and we found a wooden one, painted lime green, for ten cents.

David spent the rest of the day removing the vivid green paint, and then I painted it white. The following day he continued to fit the skirting tiles and then, once he'd finished, fixed the new toilet roll holder. A simple job; shouldn't have taken long. Took two days!

In retrospect there were a couple of things we should have done, which would not have cost much, but we didn't think of at the time. The bathroom, separate toilet and third bedroom or *cave*, didn't have windows. We should have put glass 'light borrows' above the doors so we could shut them without turning on the lights.

Also, as the bathroom is 17' long, we should have split it into two, giving us a proper utility room. Instead, we only allowed for the width of the washing machine; it would have been useful to have had a small set of shelves or a cupboard beside it.

Partly due to the time constraints when my brother was helping us, we didn't initially add many electrical sockets to the existing ones. Fortunately we were able to add some later. I have come to the conclusion that you can't have too many sockets, and there should be at least one in every bedroom that isn't in daily use and is easily accessible, for the hair dryer.

In between these little chores we entertained our neighbours and new friends on the newly extended terrace. There was a special pleasure in our friends' appreciation of our renovated garden table and comfy half-price chairs.

Aside from walking and cycling around the countryside, and taking part in both ex-pat British and French excursions, we loved going for walks in the evenings.

Our hamlet had recently acquired street lights, which were turned off at 11pm. After that, there was hardly any light pollution at all and the night sky was amazing. The stars were much easier to see than in England so we bought a chart of the constellations, and enjoyed trying to match the constellations to the plan. On warm summer evenings we would sit on the terrace, sipping something soothing, tracking the planes and satellites as they crossed the heavens, listening to the hoots of owls and the swishing of bats above our heads. Idyllic.

The street lights were particularly useful when we returned from entertainments in the *Salle des Fetes* late at night. If we knew Anna was going to be later than 11pm, when they were turned off, we would leave our outside lights on so she could see her way home. It was a small way to signal our thanks for all her help and friendship. She was suitably grateful, especially when wine had been taken.

Our friend and neighbour Andre sold his house, and English Rob moved in with his dog. Before long he acquired a kitten too. On one of David's solo visits, he heard plaintive crying and found Felix up a tree, apparently unable to climb down. Rob was not a particularly agile person so David fetched his ladder and rescued the kitten. As he grew Felix decided he liked our house; the dog wasn't always nice to him. We really appreciated the stable door as we could keep the cat out but still have ventilation on hot days.

Of course, there were also days when we were happy to have him inside with us and he made the most of them, always choosing to sit with his best friend David. Sometimes we had to carry him home so he didn't miss his tea, which the dog would eat if he wasn't there.

Anna was a great neighbour and friend. Although she was a busy lady, giving French conversation lessons, looking after her *potager* (vegetable garden) and chickens, writing poetry and visiting her many friends, both French and English, she was always helpful and hosted delightful supper parties. She also found time to switch on the electrics when she knew we were on our way, making sure there was beer in the fridge and leaving a little vase of garden flowers on the table. She was never obtrusive though, she was far too busy for that. She and I enjoyed watching Wimbledon together, complete with nibbles and a glass or three of suitably chilled wine.

One Sunday we were wandering around a street market when I saw a concrete plant trough with bunches of grapes carved in relief on the side. I casually pointed it out to David, then moved on, searching for a pestle and mortar. We always arranged to meet at the cafe for an aperitif so I wasn't worried when David went off on his own. When we got back to the car he opened the boot and said, 'Happy

Birthday,' proudly telling me he had paid 5€ for the trough, then laughed and admitted to giving another 10€ to a couple of chaps who carried it to the car for him! When we had to lift it out at home, I understood why the lads had demanded 5€ each. It looked really good on our terrace.

My bargain birthday present

TIPS AND INFORMATION

- *Remember in France the drink and drive limit is lower than in the UK. So don't risk your licence.*

- *When driving, you need to carry your vehicle paperwork at all times; also your passport, as many fluorescent vests as there are seats in the car, two breathalysers, a warning triangle, and possibly a few more items by now. Also remember to mask your headlights with appropriate shapes so your headlights don't shine into oncoming drivers' eyes as you will be driving on the OTHER side of the road.*

• *Gendarmes have the power to stop and search at will, and often pick on foreign drivers. They also issue on-the-spot-fines and will take you to your bank ATM if you don't have enough cash with you. So it is wise to obey their speed limits and other requirements carefully.*

Our hamlet, from the air

Chapter 17

It might sound from the above as though we worked all day, every day, and indeed in order to finish a task, sometimes we did. But nearly every evening after supper, we went for a walk to stretch our tired muscles. Our road followed the ridge of the valley, with fields either side. In September the hedges were full of blackberries. To our amazement we were the only people in the village who picked these delicious fruits.

About half a mile further on, there were some long low buildings which turned out to be hangers. A well mown section in a grassy field was the landing strip for the half a dozen privately owned dual-seater airplanes and microlights housed there. A couple of these planes would, for a small fee, take up a passenger, who could fly over the area taking photographs. It was a private club for aficionados of small planes, where one could also have flying lessons and – hopefully – gain a pilot's licence. We never took to the air here, but enjoyed seeing the planes having fun high above the hamlet.

Looping back towards the houses we crossed a trickle of a stream, which was home to frogs and minnows. The frogs happily croaked away all the long summer evenings. Bats not only lived in the church belfry but also in the huge walnut trees which lined the roads, and they flew low between the buildings at night time.

Coming back into the village on the other side of the valley, we passed the farm yard where chickens, ducks and dogs happily roamed between the huge tractors and farm machinery. The farmer rotated the crops; one year the fields were a burst of yellow sunflowers, the next he grew wheat, and then again we would arrive in May to find the fields the brilliant blue of linseed flowers. In September he worked in the fields until one in the morning, the tractors sporting spotlights like huge eyes as they trundled up and down, harvesting the crops.

Also in September was the Vendange. Jean-Yves owned a few lines of vines and he invited us, to join Anna and his family, to help pick the grapes. We all prayed for a good yield as we stooped between the low vines, picking clusters of grapes and gently placing them in buckets before tipping them into the trailer, which in a good year would have to make several trips back to the barn. Once the last grape had been picked, we rode in the empty trailer back to the farm. There his wife and daughters had laid out an amazing spread on long tables: quiches, salads, pastas, baskets of baguettes, cold meats and cheeses, all to be washed down by the previous year's wine. We had worked up quite an appetite under the sun, so this simple meal lasted several hours and became quite raucous. By the time we had to leave we'd forgotten we couldn't speak French.

An unoccupied house in our hamlet

In the village 'square' was the dilapidated ruin of an unoccupied house, which had been lived in by an elderly woman who had died several years earlier. The beneficiaries wanted to sell it, but the French inheritance laws are very restrictive in that when a person dies every single blood relative inherits: the spouse gets half, the children split a quarter between them, and other relatives share the remaining quarter. So if they don't agree what to do with the property, including price, then nothing happens.

On top of that, for every year that the property stands empty, it racks up habitation taxes which are then taken out of the sale price when it finally sells. This disintegrating property, left open to the elements, attracted quite a lot of interest over the years. Several British people, including some of our neighbours, tried to buy it, but every time someone made an offer, the owners upped the price, hoping to cover the growing debts. Eventually our French friends with the ex-rock 'n' roll life style, bought it. They owned the house behind it, sharing a boundary and access with it, so buying this *petit maison* made sense. As their house was also small, they used it as guest accommodation, mending the roof and installing windows (it had never had proper windows, just shutters).

I mentioned that, at the start of this venture, neither David nor I had much confidence in our French. Over the years our grasp of the language improved greatly, especially when we needed to talk with our builders. We quickly realised that they understood more English than they admitted, so be careful what you say.

We were about two years into our renovation when my French was severely tested. The local *brico* (DIY) stores had weekly special-offer leaflets which we eagerly scanned for bargains. In this way we had bought a step ladder for 10€, several internal doors at half price, extra electrical fittings, tiles and so on. One week, insulation was heavily reduced; we needed twelve rolls to cover the whole loft so asked them to deliver. While we were in the shop I noticed a tall lightweight metal ladder on special offer, so we bought that to add to the delivery. The ladder would be a godsend as our only form of access to the loft was a worm-riddled wooden ladder which had been left in the barn, and on which a couple of rungs had recently broken.

That evening we were enjoying a quiet moment on the terrace when a van screeched to a halt outside. It was the insulation. We unloaded the rolls and then asked about the ladder. The driver knew nothing about it, and anyway he was on his way home so wasn't going back to the shop to look for it. He just shrugged, French style, and jumped into the cab before tearing off in a cloud of dust.

We weren't happy. We were heading home the next day to catch the late evening ferry and needed to leave immediately after lunch. So with the car packed ready for departure, we headed to 3MMM to ask after our ladder. They all professed to not speak English nor to understand our French. We showed our receipt and asked to know where was our ladder. After much to-ing and fro-ing it transpired that the assistant hadn't put a Sold sticker on it, and another assistant had then re-sold it. It was an unrepeatable special offer and had been the last one. There was a lot of Gaelic shrugging of shoulders and eventually we were offered a credit note, which would expire in six months.

But we wouldn't be back within six months so that was no use to us. We insisted they ring around their branches to find another ladder. We argued back and forth for about an hour with both sides growing increasingly exasperated. Noon – and the store closing for lunch – was fast approaching and no resolution had been reached. We refused to leave the shop until a satisfactory solution was found. In desperation I asked if they had another ladder of the same length as we had to be able to reach the roof.

They muttered and hummed and hawed, then led us to a very sturdy three piece ladder that was double the price. It was really too heavy, I said, I wouldn't be able to carry it myself. They were desperate to get rid of us; they wanted their lunch. I asked if we could have it for the same price as the original ladder. *Non*, they said, *pas possible.* However, another shrug, they would reduce the price so we would only have to pay another 20€. It was past midday by now, and they were increasingly agitated. I suggested we would think about it over lunch and return at 2pm.

We almost thought they wouldn't re-open, but they did.

The infamous
ladder in action

Our patience and French had been taxed but we were proud of the way we had stuck to our guns. We drove back to the house for a quick sandwich before closing up and returning to the store to hand over another 20€ and arrange delivery. Thankfully when I popped across to Anna to explain the situation, she said she would open up if they rang her first (which did happen but not for another two weeks and a couple of reminding phone calls). We had to drive like the wind to catch the ferry; we did, but once again we were last on board.

Despite this problem, in this area of France the British are generally liked and held in esteem. The Charente was a hot bed of resistance during the Second World War and we met quite a few men, and women, who were proud of their part in sabotaging the German forces; they remained grateful for the help they had received from Britain. Sadly there are very few left now, but there are still many artefacts from the war adorning the walls of private houses and *caves,* as well as museums.

You might think we didn't have time to explore, but that wouldn't be true at all. We gave ourselves a strict 'working day' time limit; we rarely began work before 9.30am, sat for a proper lunch, and stopped by 6ish. Of course there were times when a task took longer and we worked into the night, but by and large we managed to pace ourselves.

We have spent ten fun-filled and enjoyable years, creating and furnishing our French barn conversion. Initially we had planned that Phase One – the ground floor – would take a year, and then Phase Two would be adding two or three bedrooms and a bathroom in the loft, which would take another year. But, as you will have realised, we were so, so wrong.   Phase One took four and a half years, and we abandoned Phase Two as we realised that not only was it completely unnecessary, but also we'd run out of money. We had the best fun doing up the barn year after year, on a very tight budget.   We spent nearly as much time searching for bargains as we did actually doing the work.

On a cycle ride one day we came across a tiny village holding a *brocante* in their miniature square. where I spied this soup tureen under a table. The stall holders didn't know how much they wanted for it; they were just clearing out *Grand-mere's* house.   I rather diffidently offered 5€, expecting them to suggest at least double. No one was more astonished than me when they agreed and helped pack it carefully into my bike basket.

The soup tureen for 5€ from a *brocante*

Our commune boasted a *Plan D'eau*, which is a man-made lake suitable for swimming, canoeing and fishing; with plenty of grassy areas and trees for picnics and a mobile pizza van in the summer. The commune also had a *Gargotte*; an open sided barn-like structure which seated about one hundred people, situated in a woodland. This also had a playground and kitchen, and anyone could hire it out for parties, evening open air concerts, etc. We were invited to several parties as well as an evening pop concert which were held there.

Our hamlet held an annual *Fete du Pain de Fort* (the bread oven fete); the villagers brought along their picnic, tables and chairs, and the local baker baked a loaf of bread for every household. Very convivial.

Garden - looking good at last

We socialised a lot. Our English neighbours had started a Quiz club which they held once a month in our *Sales des Fetes* (village hall, conveniently close to us). Ex-pats from miles around would come for the social chat, the brain teasing quiz, the home cooked curry and a bottle of plonk. We never won but sometimes claimed the 'wooden spoon'.

One interesting way to get to know the area was to search out the cafes and restaurants the French frequent. Lunches were cheaper than evening meals and many small towns sport a restaurant which offered a cheap set menu.

When we bought our house, these would just be a few tables in someone's house, and *Madam* would cook whatever came to hand that day. A basket of baguettes would be refilled as soon as it emptied. Then a little bowl of beautifully dressed crisp lettuce would be brought. The main course, often gammon and chips or *haricot vert* (green beans) would be followed by a cheese board and then a choice of desserts. You could buy a bottle of very decent wine or go for *un pichet* (carafe) of the local *vin de table*. My favourite pudding was *mousse au chocolate* but that was everyone's favourite; you had to arrive dead on noon to be in with a chance.

Anna started a group for English and French people to meet and mingle. She gave French lessons in her house once a week, and also arranged coach trips. One month we visited the museum and craft studios in nearby Tusson, followed by a slap-up lunch in the local restaurant; another month the group hired a coach and we visited the *Cadre Noir* in Saumur, which for me was a great treat as I am well and truly into horses. On that occasion we lunched in an underground restaurant where wines had been hidden in the caves during the war.

A sweet shop in Saumur

After lunch we had time to wander around the town which has an island around which the river Seine runs. Hidden alleys led to small squares were we came across the most delicious smelling sweet and chocolate shop. Naturally we had to go in, but choosing what to buy was incredibly hard.

Randonees (walks) were regularly organised around the beautiful countryside which again, always ended in a restaurant for lunch. Each walk was organised around a different village and there were usually up to twenty friendly people taking exercise while having a good time. One week we followed the orchid trail through a wood; another week the walk included crossing a pretty stream on a flat-bottomed boat, pulling ourselves over by a rope.

Yet another excursion saw us on the *Velo-Train* which starts at Confolens. If you have ever watched the old Keystone Cops movies you'll remember when a couple of men frantically pumped a trolley along the rail tracks. The *Velo-train* was a bit like that except we sat and pedalled. Each trolley could seat four people with two pedalling and two resting. The track is about 10 kilometres long and you alight at the end for a refreshing coffee or ice cream. Then you make the return trip. Our lunch time destination on this occasion was beside a nearby *Plan D'eau*. This particular one sported a proper cafe, a fountain, a sandy beach and a children's play area. Great fun but I lost my wedding ring which was a shame.

The area is full of Roman remains: there is an open air amphitheatre near the town of Rouillac which is a good day out. Chassenon has Roman thermal baths which are worth a visit. Dolmans abound in fields, and there are several small vineyards and museums. On top of these, there are the monthly markets - Rouillac has a particularly large one, with livestock too.

My favourite way to spend a Sunday was to trawl around the *brocantes* (car boot sales). There are several types; *brocantes* have the best quality items; the ones held at Tusson and Civray are particularly well attended and have hundreds of stalls. *Vide Greniers* sell items from attics; these are more likely to be held in smaller villages once a year. Then occasionally there is a *Vide de Village*, which doesn't mean the village is for sale. Everyone in the village/hamlet has a table top sale in their front garden. The village hires a burger van and visitors wander from house to house, buying and having a quick nosey around the gardens and homes. Very sociable and enlightening.

Most areas in France also produce local English language newsletters and magazines, offering a selection of recipes, stories, crosswords, children's page and adverts for pretty much everything, from an IT expert to a second hand tractor. In the south there are English speaking radio stations which mirror the local stations we have here in England. Some towns, such as nearby Ruffec, show an English film with French subtitles once a month in the local cinema. Our area also had a pet charity where you could buy or donate English books too.

Relaxing - hedge grown, garden tidy
Chapter 18

We were visiting our son in Australia one spring when an invoice arrived in my e-mail, from the couple who tend our garden while we're away. It nearly gave me a heart attack.

My first thought was 'gosh, that's a lot of euros for mowing the grass'; I always read the bottom line first, don't you? Then I scanned the blurb which led to my second thought: 'no one told us our house had suffered storm and flood damage or talked to us about insurance.'

Then, at last, I read the heading – it wasn't our house, not our damage – they'd sent someone else's invoice by mistake. Phew. What a relief. I had to have a quick restorative to stop my hands from shaking. Fortunately I like Australian wines.

My subsequent thoughts were sympathy for the unfortunate owners of the flooded property, and what they could have done to possibly prevent said problems. Which in turn has prompted me to add some suggestions on how to winterise empty houses. After all there must be hundreds (well, quite a lot) of people who, like us, spend the spring and summer months in France then shut up their houses for the cold, wet winters. As a child I lived in a stone farmhouse in England; my family later had boats which had to be protected during the winter, so I have brought this hard won knowledge to our converted barn and am happy to report that, touch wood, we didn't have any problems with burst pipes, dampness, mould or bad smells; nor did it sink.

The secret to avoiding nasty smells and pockets of damp is ventilation. We have purposely chosen furniture with legs rather than low material bases which touch the floor. If you already have divan beds or soft furnishings with low bases, before you leave lift them off the floor (a brick, not wood, under each leg will suffice), so the air can circulate underneath. I also move furniture, such as bookcases, away from outside walls – just a few inches – for the same reason, and take up rugs and any other materials such as long curtains. Leave cupboard and room doors open, so air can circulate.

I make sure I wash the floors several days before we depart, and only sweep the tiles on the last day so the air inside the house is dry. I cover lampshades with old towels or carrier bags to avoid fly droppings, but I no longer bother with dust sheets everywhere; no movement in the empty house means no dust is generated.

The major problem in winter is cold getting into water pipes. Where it's possible, lag the pipes – those spongy tube things are good – or tuck them under the insulation. If the pipes are hidden in walls or under the floor, the answer is to empty them. Turn the water off at the mains (where the meter is, probably next to the road) and then open the taps until the water stops flowing. No need to leave the taps open but don't put the basin plugs in. Empty the toilet cisterns by flushing after the water has been turned off. The 'out' pipes should be ok, any water in the toilet bowls can expand if it freezes and the down pipes should all have flowed down into the fosse (septic tank).

Make sure you remember to insulate, turn off and drain the garden tap too.

I mentioned earlier in this book about choosing a sensible position for your hot water tank; but if your hot water tank is vulnerable to external frosts, drain some water out of it so there is enough empty space for expansion should it freeze. By vulnerable I mean if it touches the floor, is in an un-insulated space such as the roof, or against an outside wall. (On our plumber's advice, ours was in the centre of the barn, hanging on the wall next to the bathroom, where it was well protected from outside temperatures) Make sure there is a tap under the tank which will drain the water (into buckets or bowls) as once the mains are turned off, there's no pressure to send the water along to the taps.

To reduce the risk of fire, unplug everything from the sockets and turn off the electricity at the meter. If you have a land phone line, organise to have it switched off while you're away so you don't have to pay the standing charge. Also remember to shut off any gas bottles.

Having made sure you haven't left any perishables around and have wedged the fridge and freezer doors open (you did defrost them last night, didn't you?) lock all the windows, doors and shutters, and leave a key with a neighbour/friend who will check periodically that all is well with your beloved home while you're away.

TIPS AND INFORMATION

- *Think ahead. Ok, you only plan to use it as a holiday home, but life has a habit of kicking you in the teeth. You might find you have to rent it out, or perhaps live in it permanently. Or even to sell. So, think about what will be needed if you were living in the house permanently, ie, washing machine, tumble drier, dish washer, central heating, etc.*

- *Whatever you do, try and keep a toe-hold in your home country. French properties don't increase in value the way UK properties do, so if you sell everything in the UK, when/if you need to return you'll probably find yourself priced out of the market.*

- *Do leave a key with someone you trust. Ask them to look in every so often to just check on the plumbing and possible water ingress. Give them your details so they can e-mail you (at no cost to them). Either pay them in cash or bring them goodies from the UK that they can't get in France. Our neighbours liked porridge oats, cheddar cheese which hadn't been frozen, curry powder, and hot cross buns.*

- *Make sure your insurance covers the property even when it's left unoccupied for long periods of time.*

Sunset from the terrace

CHAPTER 19

I started the last chapter with 'while visiting our son in Australia...', which just goes to show how planning for the future can't be set in stone. We had spent several years working on our own little bit of France, enjoying the slower pace of life and having friends visit. We loved showing off our home and taking our guests to some of the local hot spots, improving our language skills, making friends, entertaining and taking part in the local village festivities.

We thought our children would come for holidays, but they didn't. Our daughter said it was too quiet, she wanted somewhere with a beach, nightlife and young people. One son had small children and couldn't cope with the long drive, and the other son met an Australian lass and followed her back to Oz. Other family members either had their own holiday places in various countries, or weren't keen to travel so far, although David's parents did fly out a couple of times. The cost of running two homes (one in the UK) was mounting, and on top of that, we now needed to save up to fly to Australia occasionally.

There was an advert on TV where the girl asks her little sister which she likes more, Daddy or chips? Well, that became our dilemma. Australia or France? We knew we would be holidaying in Australia more than France and sadly we couldn't do both. Each time we asked the question, the answer came out as Australia. So, after much soul searching and heart ache – after all, that house was the culmination of many years of dreaming and contained huge amounts of our blood, sweat and tears – we decided to sell.

We didn't reach this decision overnight; we spent many weeks agonising over the way forwards, with first me and then David justifying our conclusion.

Many cups of tea, and glasses of wine, were consumed as we researched alternatives. We asked several agents to value our barn conversion but even after we put it on the market, we weren't totally committed. Thankfully by the time we had an offer we had reconciled ourselves to selling.

Selling in France is very different from the UK system. Most *Immobiliers* have multi-lingual agents so they can cater for both French and foreign buyers. Agents charge approximately 30% of your asking price, which, because the purchaser pays it, is added to the advertised purchase price.

In France, full surveys are carried out at the vendor's expense. The *Immobilier* will encourage you to authorise these as soon as the house is put on the market, but beware as some only last a year and all have to be re-done if the property hasn't sold within two years. Electric and water surveys will be carried out by the respective utilities; then you will need specialists for woodworm, termite, bat, ground pollution, septic tank, and anything else they can think of. Your agent will organise these for you.

Once you have accepted an offer, the purchaser has a two week period of grace during which to change their mind, after which they are expected to sign the preliminary papers and pay a deposit. However if your buyer is canny (or French) this period can be extended indefinitely by one excuse after another: an unsatisfactory or incomplete survey, unable to attend the notaire's office, etc. So never count your chickens. We had three sales fall through, one even on the day completion was supposed to take place. (That made us very cross as we'd flown out especially to attend).

If the price offered is lower than you need, you might be able to negotiate with the agent to reduce their fee so you still get your required price. Also, in France, the purchaser pays both agent's and *Notaire*'s fees.

When you set your sale figure, remember you may have to pay Capital Gains Tax on completion. Although French property prices don't increase the way that British ones do, hopefully all your hard work will have raised its value as well as making it easier to sell. Collect all your work invoices and receipts so you can add them to the original purchase price, in order to claim against the CGT. Note however that any items purchased by you in the UK are not included; nor are items bought in France and installed by yourselves.

(We couldn't claim for our kitchen as we'd fitted it ourselves). The only invoices which count are those issued by SIRET registered companies. It's as well to remember this when you are tempted to use *sur le noir* (on the black) workmen.

So, your purchaser has signed the initial paperwork, the surveys are in and satisfactory, and you have a completion date. Now all you have to do is work out what furniture you want to take home, and what you need to sell. There are numerous English magazines in which you can advertise; also the *Emmaus* charity will take many items, especially good things, but of course they don't pay you for them. We were fortunate that our agent had just sold a couple of houses which were being furnished as gites, so these new owners bought a lot of our furniture – beds, chairs, tables, and so on.

If you want to bring large items back to UK, you'll need to find a man with a van. This might not be easy now, as the French government has clamped down on what they realised was a lucrative source of income, and started taxing enterprising van-owners. We left some non-perishable things in a friend's barn, which we collected the following year.

The concrete flower trough was too heavy to take back to UK in our car. Both Anna and Rob said we could leave it in their gardens until it could be collected. Between us, David and I managed to lift it into the wheelbarrow.

"Where are we going to take it?' David asked. "To Anna or to Rob?'

Anna lived uphill from us, and Rob was downhill. I grabbed the handles.

"Downhill of course. Just don't expect me to bring it back if he's not in.'

Eventually a friend had it brought back with her furniture when she relocated to the UK.

TIPS AND INFORMATION

• *In our experience, it's worth giving careful consideration to how realistic it is that your friends and family will come to stay. It may be that you don't need the property to be as big as you think.*

• *This bears repeating: The only invoices which count are those issued by SIRET registered companies. It's as well to remember this when you are tempted to use unregistered workmen.*

- *When a property changes hands, the septic tank has to be emptied and any chimneys swept. Your Immobilier will organise surveyors.*

- *If your kitchen units are free-standing, you can take them with you.*

SAYING GOODBYE WAS PAINFUL
CHAPTER 20

We spent ten fun-filled and enjoyable years living our
French dream.   Nearly everything we bought was
second hand or given to us as presents. Even knowing
we had nowhere to put things, it was really hard to part
with any of it. David was more ruthless than I, but even
so, we now have dozens of boxes of 'stuff' in our loft.
Some was brought home knowing our daughter would
need equipment for her new flat; other things I simply
couldn't bear to part with.   We had accumulated over
200 books and I sent at least half to a charity shop.

I still haven't unpacked all the ones I brought home, which goes to show I should have parted with even more. It's important to weigh up the cost of hiring a van to bring items back, against their actual worth.

We sometimes wish we had brought more favourite things home, but we are already over-furnished, and it was important to reduce the stress of selling to a manageable level.

Now we watch with great delight and recognition such programmes as Escape to the Country (France) and Escape to the Chateau, DIY; these send David trawling through the internet for properties for sale, and some are really enticing. He is keen on plots with a view, on which we could build from scratch, or perhaps a remote stone house; I would prefer a pre-fab wooden chalet.

But we're a lot older now and wouldn't want to take on so much work. We realised our dream, we made a really good job of our barn, albeit small in comparison with other peoples' renovations, and we were sad to have to sell. We'd do it again in a heartbeat given half a chance; the whole experience has been a huge 'enabler'; allowing us to go on to modernise and renovate homes here in UK. The experience and skills we learned widened our horizons; we made new friends and have lots of happy memories.

Although we dropped the asking price, we made enough profit to have to pay Capital Gains Tax. We also had many wonderful — if sometimes exhausting — holidays at little cost. Somehow French rain and snow didn't seem so dispiriting as bad weather in the UK, and the sunny days seemed endless, just like our childhood memories. We loved improving our French, meeting new people, and of course enjoying the food and wine. When we sold, *Mnsr le Maire* shook David by the hand (I was awarded three kisses, French style, on the cheeks) and said that our hard work had enhanced the village and we would be greatly missed.

If we hadn't sold our lovely barn we wouldn't have had all the joy of visiting our son and his new family in Australia. A dream can become a reality; but it doesn't have to last forever. We've had to move on a bit sooner than we anticipated, but that hasn't detracted from our achievement. We still visit France, staying with friends and exploring new areas, but now we are also learning about Australia and clocking up the air miles!

If this book has inspired you to follow your dreams, whatever they may be, I wish you well. We learned a lot about DIY and even more about ourselves. We had fun and laughter, sometimes frustration and tears, but we can truthfully say creating our beautiful French home was one of the best experiences of our lives.

Printed in Poland
by Amazon Fulfillment
Poland Sp. z o.o., Wrocław